Eager Spring

Published by Barfield Press

Other books by Owen Barfield:

Night Operation
The Rose on the Ash-Heap
This Ever Diverse Pair

Forthcoming new editions:

The Silver Trumpet
Orpheus: A Poetic Drama
The Case for Anthroposophy
Short stories
Poetry

www.owenbarfield.org

Owen Barfield

Eager Spring

Barfield Press

Series Editor: Dr. Jane Hipolito

Published by Barfield Press UK
First Published, 2008
This Second Edition, 2009

A catalogue record for this book is available from
the British Library.

Eager Spring by Owen Barfield
ISBN 978-0-9559582-0-5

Printed on paper with Sustainable Forestry Initiative (SFI)
accreditation.

Produced on behalf of
the Owen Barfield Literary Estate.

The Literary Estate promotes and safeguards the works
and intellectual legacy of Arthur Owen Barfield.

Ò`B

www.owenbarfield.org

INTRODUCTION

This is a tale both contemporary and timeless. Written in the mid-1980s, it addresses many of the same themes and concerns which were the cornerstones of Barfield's writings for over six decades, yet with a freshness of approach rarely found in an author approaching his 90th year. As Barfield himself observed, his works show remarkable unity of theme; what has always made him such an important author is not just the depth and originality of his thought but the variety of its expression.

Poems, plays, Platonic dialogues, lectures, literary essays, novels, märchen: all are expressions of a coherent philosophy, but Barfield manages always to approach his subject so as to cast new light upon it. He is perhaps the only one of the Inklings who truly deserves the honorific of *philosopher*, but he is also equally a storyteller. The delight in reading one's first Barfield is in the introduction to his thought (I know of no other author who so invariably forces his readers to *think*); that in reading a second, and third, and fourth, is in sharing his exploration of new ground. You do not so much agree with him as realize, under the stimulus of his example, that most of your assumptions about language, history, perception, consciousness, reality, and a host of other topics are uncritical almost to the point of naiveté.

What kind of story, then, is *Eager Spring*? It is many things at once, a remarkably complex story for such a short book. On one level it is the story — albeit obliquely — of Barfield's conception of human history and the changes which have occurred, both inner and outer, due to the evolution of consciousness. But it is also much more than that: it is the story of a marriage under stress like that of John and Margaret in *English People* (Barfield's major work of fiction, written more than fifty years before and still unpublished), an estrangement caused by one partner's attempt to follow up an interest which the other finds meaningless. It is also the story of an apt student finding an apt teacher, like Burgeon, Barfield's persona, in his masterpiece, *Unancestral Voice*; the astonished impact the discovery of a writer's work at just the right time in your life can have on expanding your whole horizon of thought, whether Lewis's MacDonald, Tolkien's Morris, or Barfield's Steiner. It is the story of someone trying to keep up an intellectually stimulating inner life under the grind of daily commitments and the discouragement of having no one with whom to share one's hard-won insights (again, like Burgeon, but this time as he appears in the delightful semi-autobiographical fiction of *This Ever-Diverse Pair*). Perhaps underlying all these things, it is the story of the struggle between good and evil, between death and the forces which affirm life. The latter are represented here by the figure of Harry Coppard, a man determined to spend his life giving back to the earth a little of what his steel-smelting ancestors have taken from it, an arborer whose life's work reaches its fulfilment near the end of the book when the downlands where he lives are reforested and a small local spring — the 'eager spring' of the title — flows again for the first time in centuries.

But where there is life there is death, and good, evil; Michael has his Ahriman;   for Barfield, like Blake, understands polarities. If the forces of evil in this story are more amorphous, less personalized than those of good, it is perhaps because such tends to be our daily experience: we can each identify people we know or believe to be kind, self-sacrificing, generous, or loving, but the whole trend of modern religion, medicine, and justice has been away from identifying individuals with evil, so that when a politician refers to his rivals as 'an evil empire' it is hard for us to take it as anything other than mere rhetoric. We want a Heaven, but denigrate the idea of a Hell. But for Barfield, evil exists, and the forces which deny life in this book take a frighteningly realistic and modern form: *biocides*. As a scholar of words, the author of not only *Speaker's Meaning* and *History in English Words* but the seminal *Poetic Diction*, Barfield here avoids the vagueness of 'hazardous by-products' or 'chemical wastes' (or even the apparent neutrality of 'pesticides' and 'herbicides') and thus forces us to see them for what they are: *bio-cides*, killers of life.

The ecological bent of this novella is something quite new to Barfield's work. But it is deeply characteristic of Barfield that even when he is most revealing of participation in modern concerns — deforestation in the Amazon, the proliferation of biocides — he puts them in perspective with their historical antecedents: on the small shelf of books in Harry Coppard's cottage we find "a Ruskin, a Richard Jeffries, a Thoreau, Schumacher's *Guide to the Perplexed*, and ... certainly Rachel Carson's *Silent Spring*", the cornerstones of the movement our heroine is in the end forced to embrace. For above all else this is the story of a thinker moved inexorably into "the need for action and the obligation to take it", and the steps whereby Vi's postgraduate inquiry into the relationship between myth and allegory and the nature of courtly love leads her into involvement as an ecological activist are both psychologically convincing and true to life. What began as a mental journey eventually becomes — as any deep inquiry into human history must — a spiritual one as well. But knowledge, and wisdom, are for Barfield things which must be shared, and it is the deeds, not just the intellectual journeying, which make her not just this novel's protagonist but its heroine.

Throughout the story Vi is thinking of writing a book about her research, a sort of *Allegory of Love*, but when we and her husband finally come to read it as she lies poised between life and death, we find instead of a learned tome, 'Virginia's Conte', a *märchen* or myth-allegory (in Barfield's view it is a false dichotomy to divide the two) which comprises the final third of this book.

Some readers will perhaps prefer the fairytale to the realistic novella which gives rise to it. Others will enjoy Barfield's uncannily accurate portrayal of the life of today's graduate student and fledgling academic or his quiet look at modern love, in which a couple are friends, then lovers, then roommates before they become man and wife. Still others will appreciate the dynamic contrast between the two parts, as two tales — one realistic and contemporary, the other fantastic and timeless, but both telling the same story — are brought together into a single whole.

This then is *Eager Spring*. For those who have never read Owen Barfield before, this is a good place to start.

Those returning to a favourite author may be in for an
unexpected surprise and pleasure, for Barfield shares with
us here some of the insights he gained in his long life.
Barfield had a great affinity and talent for fiction;   a
modern realistic fiction not unlike E.M. Forster's but
charged with mythic overtones particularly his own. He
has been neglected by readers of his fellow Inklings largely
I think because he did not publish a significant body of
fiction embodying his ideas as had Williams, Lewis, and
Tolkien.   Thus we should welcome *Eager Spring* for
redressing the balance, but most of all because it is, quite
simply, one of the best things he has ever written.

John D. Rateliff

CHAPTER I

"I'LL TELL YOU what, why don't we have a look at Eager Spring before we go on up?"

It was a Sunday morning in June, very early, as the sun was only just above the horizon, and the two graduate students from the redbrick university of Cartishall were on their way up to the downs. Leonard Brook, who had just put the question, was studying archaeology and Virginia (or Vi, as everyone called her) Fisher had graduated with honours in English literature. The idea was to spend the long summer day, part walking and part lazing, on Fraxon Down, the long hogsback of a hill that looked down on Cartishall from a mile or two away. Though neither of them had ever bothered to find it, they knew that at the foot of the slope, not far from the footpath, were the remains of a spring, long since run dry but once poetically named and carefully tended. So they turned aside from the path with the help of Leonard's large-scale Ordnance map and, after pushing their way through a good deal of brambly undergrowth, came on what they were looking for.

Not just a nondescript hole in the ground, or crack in a miniature limestone escarpment; here, badly crumbled with age but still impressively distinct from — and yet somehow perfectly at home in — its surroundings, was the large stone head of a lion, from whose open mouth had formerly issued the water that had scooped that shallow stony bed beneath it. They stood looking at it in silence. Its own silence seemed to speak to them, and for a moment even the thought of the glad day before them — the blue sky above, the wide expanse of gorse and heather, and underfoot the springy turf occasionally starred with peeping flowers — became focused in the stone image. Then, without speaking, they made their way back to the footpath.

"How long should you say it is since there was any water there, Leo?" asked his companion after they had walked on a few steps.

"I don't know; not less than two hundred years, I should think."

"And why should it have run dry?"

"Not much doubt about that. Deforestation. All this upland was once covered with trees."

"What difference did that make?"

The study of archaeology entails more than a smattering of geology and its allied subjects, and there was — or Vi felt there was — a hint of complacent didacticism in Leo's reply.

"The roots lead the rainwater down into the soil and give it a chance to seep down to a solid stratum that acts as a water table. Take them away and the water runs off. Especially as, without the shelter of the leaves, the soil cakes and hardens and the rain never gets a chance to soak in. It runs off or evaporates."

Vi Fisher and Leo Brook had been fellow students for three years and, for the last year, rather more than that. They were 'going steady', as it was then called, and they shared an unspoken supposition that some day they would marry. Perhaps for that reason each was hypersensitive to nuances of behaviour and tones of voice in the other. Leo was a darling, there was no doubt about that, but somehow Vi didn't quite like the feeling of being 'taught'. Was there a touch of masculine condescension there? Certainly she didn't know much about the earth and its doings, but she was as knowledgeable about other things as he was about all that. She knew a lot about the Middle Ages, for instance, and her proposal for a thesis on allegory had been accepted without hesitation. She stopped herself from asking her 'tutor' the question on the tip of her tongue — why were the trees cut down? — and cast about in her mind instead.

Ah! She remembered: iron.

"I believe the greater part of England was once covered with forest," she said, "and they began cutting the trees down for iron-smelting."

"Not only that, my dear" (as knowledgeable as ever), "the charcoal-burners had been at them already, and the growing demand for iron, when it came later, just increased the tempo. And of course all the time plenty of them were being taken for cooking and house-warming, not to mention shipbuilding."

To chasten and suppress a faint residue of irritation, she took his arm, and at once forgot it. Fraxon Down was more like an undulating expanse of moorland than like the "blunt, bow-headed, hump-backed downs" of Sussex, and it was not so very high. Before long they had crested the last slope, and there was nothing above them but sky. They stood still and looked at the world. They had both been there before, but neither of them at that virginal hour that succeeds the dawn. For a few moments Vi had the strange

impression that she had never before realised light, never
tasted it, so to speak, as she was doing now. Near at hand
a few drops of dew still glistened on patches of wiry grass-
blades; and the very air seemed to be glistening above the
wide expanse of heather, bracken, furze and bog-myrtle
that led the eye out over the level countryside between and
on to the distant hills that bounded the horizon.
Glistening? Or was it she herself who was — tingling?
Flooded with the joy of it she felt a strong impulse to share
with Leo by kissing him, but she checked that for fear any
change would destroy the wonder of it. Time enough for
that later, when they would be sitting down together to eat
the primitive victuals they had agreed would suffice for
breakfast. Nothing whatever had happened, and yet she
was to recall those few vivid moments from time to time
during the rest of her life.

   They walked on, keeping mainly to the high ground,
and soon found a suitable spot for rest and breakfast. By
now the magic morning light had hardened into the light
of common day — common only by contrast, for it was
certainly a glorious day. Their conversation was mainly
of the sporadic kind that a walk in the open encourages,
because there is plenty to take in from outside. Fellow
students, professional foibles, comparisons between their
respective family lives cropped up as islands in a sea of
companionable silence. Nor did they fear occasionally
touching on 'shop', for both were keen students. Indeed,
Leo's archaeological bent was partly responsible for the
direction they were taking towards a large hollow or cup
in the hills, where he had heard there were formations that

suggested the possibility of prehistoric earthworks. He rather wanted to see what he thought of them.

Vi's interests were less remote, though they too were historical. If you had asked her why she had chosen to specialise in the medieval period, she would probably have said she didn't quite know. Actually it was due to a late twentieth-century critic whose writings especially appealed to her. Her own notions anent the relation between allegory and myth, her literary hero's principal subject, and the Romantics' error in insisting on a categorical gulf between them, were as yet so unformed that she was reluctant to allude to them. But she sensed that, since mythology and archaeology both point to pre-history, a realm existed where her own and Leo's respective fields of study — which the University insisted on dignifying with the name of 'research' — marched with one another.

By about midday, after a good deal of walking and a good deal of lying on their backs looking up at the sky, they reached the lip of the hollow and paused there to eat the lunch they had brought with them. This was followed by a long rest, at close quarters, in the heather.

At last they decided it was time to move. They stood up side by side looking down into the hollow. Not a very deep one, it was nevertheless low enough for seeing over the tops of the oak and beech with which it was generously wooded. Leo found himself recalling a day on holiday in Switzerland. He had stood gazing down — only then it was from a mountain slope, above the glacial level — across a valley a thousand and more feet below, sombre indeed by contrast with the liquid light all about him, but

somehow soothingly alive beneath its dark green carpet of
secretive conifers.

"Not much sign of earthworks from here," he said, "I
expect —"

"Look!" Vi interrupted him, "smoke!" She was right.
A wisp of smoke was rising from a spot somewhere among
the trees and trailing horizontally over them as if reluctant
to disperse.

"That's odd," she added. "Can there be a cottage
there? I thought all this was common land."

"So did I. Some sort of ancient customary tenure, I
suppose. Come on, let's go down." And very soon they
were among the trees, walking in the direction from which
they had seen the smoke rising. It was not long before they
caught a glimpse through the trees of a steep-ridged roof,
tiled with the old red tiles that favour the growth of golden
lichen. Now they were in the glade where the cottage stood
and could see how that roof bulged and dipped. But there
were no missing tiles. Old it might be, but not neglected.
From beneath its broad eaves there peeped — or so it
seemed because of its unusual height and steepness — a
few small windows with small leaded panes that looked as
though they were made for peering out at the world rather
than for lighting the interior. Approaching the back of the
house, they observed a neatly kept plot of vegetables, some
bean poles and, a little to the side, three beehives in a sunny
position. Walking round to the front they found a plank
bench beside the door and turned instinctively to see what
the unknown resident would contemplate when he sat
there. The trees divided, opening up a southerly view over

forest and fields and admitting a weedgrown and potholed lane, which seemed to be the only approach — at all events for vehicles — to the cottage. Whether or not neolithic man or iron-age man had ever lived up here, it was an enchanting place on a June day, with a whisper of a breeze in the branches above and no other sound but that of an occasional bee homing into its hive.

"Fascinating!" It was Vi who broke the silence.

"Yes, but the fact remains that I'm devilish thirsty. That tomato was not enough. We ought to have brought drinks."

"Too heavy to carry."

"Why not knock and ask them for a glass of water?"

"All right. *You* do it."

But Leo's first tentative, then vigorous knocking evoked no response. 'They' were evidently out.

"Shall we go on?"

"No. Find somewhere to sit and wait 'til they come back — as long as they're not too long about it."

They sat leaning against the fence, ancient but in tolerably good repair, that enclosed the little garden, and faced a track leading into the glade from another direction. They were lucky. It was not long before they saw a male figure approaching.

'Let's hope this is the owner," said Leo, and Vi:

"I wonder what he does. He can't be a shepherd because there aren't any sheep." She had noticed that he carried what looked like a long stick that might have been a crook. But as he neared, she saw that it was in fact a rigid iron bar sharpened to a point at the bottom end.

From his left hand there dangled a small empty sack. They had time to observe his face before they addressed him — ruddy as a peasant's but with a pattern of lines on it that were the reverse of bucolic. He looked to be somewhere around fifty years old.

As soon as they told him their need he invited them in, and they found themselves sitting with a jug of water and two large mugs in a low-sided room, larger than you would expect and obviously serving as both living-room and kitchen. The well they had seen in the garden explained, with their thirst, why that water tasted so good.

The room was very simply furnished — plates, cups and saucers on a dresser; a wood-burning stove; no television or radio, as far as they could see; and a single shelf of books. The shelf was too far away for Vi to see the titles or the authors' names with certainty, but she thought she detected a Ruskin, a Richard Jeffries, a Thoreau, Schumacher's *Guide for the Perplexed*, and yes — that was certainly Rachel Carson's *Silent Spring*. The man seemed in no hurry to talk. It was clear that he was the sole occupant of the cottage. Perhaps he lived so much alone that he was not used to talking? Overtures from Leo along the lines of "You must find it very lonely living here" evoked polite discouraging responses — discouraging further questions, but not unfriendly. On the contrary. Discussing it afterwards they concluded that, all the time they were there, he had been quietly forming an impression of them — and that it was not an unfavourable one. When they had risen to take their leave, Leo, in a last desperate bid at communication, had expressed curiosity about the purpose of the pointed iron rod. In response their host had stood silently regarding them for several seconds and then, "Come and see me again some time," he had said.

As they climbed to the down again; Leo at last broke the silence. "What did you make of him?"

"A strange set-up. What does he *do*?"

"Did you notice the large wooden box in the corner? I wonder what he keeps in it."

"I know," said Vi, "I peeped."

"And what's in it?"

"Acorns."

"Are you sure?"

"Certain."

"Well that doesn't make him any less mysterious. *Why?* He certainly doesn't keep pigs, or we should have seen them."

"Yes, and probably smelt them."

With that the topic seemed for the time to have been exhausted, and the rest of the day passed as planned, with a leisurely return to Cartishall and academia. For the short remainder of that term they were both kept busy, and it was not until they returned to College in the autumn that they again took up the subject, and Leo remarked:

"One thing that keeps puzzling me is that iron rod he was carrying. What's it for?"

"Well he did invite us to come back, you remember."

So they took him at his word. There is no need to describe their visit to the cottage or the one or two that followed it. What matters is what he told them about himself and his occupation. And that was pretty nearly everything. Apparently during that brief pregnant silence, he had decided to disclose to those two young things, if they wanted it, what he had long been keeping a secret from the world.

His name was Harry Coppard, and he was the scion of a wealthy family in the industrial north. His father, a successful manufacturer of electrical hardware, astutely foreseeing the winds of change, had concentrated production more and more on electronics, and when the computer explosion arrived, his son was able to cash in on its profitable early stage before cutthroat competition had begun murdering prices. By that time he and Harry's elder brother had amassed a substantial fortune, and Harry Coppard had become a gentleman of modestly independent means.

Harry was finding, as he had guessed, a not unsympathetic audience in the two humanities students, as he went on to describe his thoughts when he had to face the decision whether to join his brother in the family business and in the world, as he saw it, into which he had grown up. Everywhere he saw technological discovery accelerating a commercial rat-race and spreading a mechanized environment. He had opted out.

He had deliberately cut himself off from everything that was going on in the publicized and advertised world, yet he had felt no inclination to join any of the drop-out communities. What he did feel was a powerful urge to *do* something, almost anything, provided it worked in the opposite direction to all that was conspicuously happening around <u>him</u>.   He had sought and found this isolated cottage.

"But is just living alone in this cottage really 'doing' anything?" Vi had asked.

And then it came out. Instead of answering, he went to the wooden box in the corner and took out two handfuls of acorns. He came back, set them in a little heap on the bare table between them, and began to sort them out, examining them one by one.

"<u>What I have been doing for the last five years</u>," he said, "<u>and what I propose to go on doing, is to plant as many acorns as I can, over as wide an area as I can, in my bit of England. I choose the ones with the fewest blemishes on them</u>."

Taken by surprise, neither of them could think of anything to say; so he added: "They have to be sunk to the proper depth, otherwise they get eaten, and I use the rod for that."

He went on to tell them how so much of the soil round there was 'scrub land', because it had once been forest — good for nothing but weeds. Not even for grazing sheep. But he saw no reason why it shouldn't one day be forest again. Then he explained how he had taken the trouble to learn something of the different qualities of soil in the neighbourhood — often evidenced by the kind of vegetation — and how he was selecting the most favourable areas for his experiment, if that was the right word for it. He had already covered a substantial area, some five hundred acres, but had not yet reached the part of the down they had walked over.

planting trees (margin note)

Again they hardly knew what to say. "Would you like to accompany me?" he asked, "I haven't done my afternoon's stint yet." They nodded assent, and he emptied the selected acorns into his little sack, which already contained some, took up the rod, and led the way up the slope in a direction opposite to the one they had approached from.

"They don't all come up, of course," he said, as they reached the top of the hollow, "but enough of them do to make it worthwhile."

Soon they were walking carefully over an unfrequented and bare-backed part of the down, from which, at irregular intervals, tiny oaks were sprouting, some with an autumn leaf or two still clinging to them. Not long after they were again on barren downland. Here Coppard stopped. He took an acorn out of the bag, struck his iron rod into the soil, and dropped the acorn into the hole, closing it loosely with his foot. This process was repeated at intervals during the rest of the walk.

Recovered by now from their initial surprise, the two students questioned him, not unsympathetically, about his motive and expectations. By the time they returned to the cottage, they had extracted with difficulty from his taciturnity or his shyness the simple pragmatic philosophy by which he had chosen to shape his life. For centuries past humanity had been despoiling the earth for its own purposes. But the earth was a living creature, and living creatures can die. It was time for man to start giving back to the earth as well as taking from it, and he, Harry Coppard, was a man. Very well, he would do his bit of giving back and, as far as he was concerned, he would begin at the beginning. The spoliation had begun, in this particular part of the world, with the cutting down of trees for smelting iron, so he was beginning there by putting them back again.

He had added, in a hesitant and almost shamefaced way, that he was rather glad to be doing it with the help of iron, the very substance for which the trees had once been sacrificed.

Puzzled but somehow deeply, even uncomfortably, impressed by so much eccentricity, Leo and Vi were mostly silent during their walk back to the College. They both felt a reluctance to discuss or argue about their experience and were content to agree that they must certainly visit the cottage again.

As indeed they did. By the time they left Cartishall at the end of the summer term, acquaintance had blossomed into friendship, and they knew how much they would miss their occasional encounters with that odd companion.

"I don't know what it is," said Vi as they were returning from their final visit. "It's not so much anything he *says*. I've never felt so entirely at peace with anyone. Not even with you."

She spoke without thinking, and had no idea how accurate she had been. She could not know as yet how deeply the impact of Coppard, his cottage, and his chosen vocation had penetrated her — had, for good or ill, implanted a second guiding impulse in her life.

CHAPTER II

DURING THE NEXT few years the life lived by Leonard Brook and Virginia Fisher was much the same as that of many other English couples of about their age. Although they had left the University, they had still to complete the required research and then to finish and present their theses for the doctorates they were aiming at. Meanwhile they subsisted on student grants from the government, supplemented by occasional assistance from their parents. The narrow margin left them for expenditure on amusements, or indeed on anything beyond necessities, did not trouble them much. Both were essentially serious-minded young people interested in studies primarily for their own sake and secondarily for the rewards that some degree of success might be expected to secure later on. Access to libraries and museums being among their requirements, they debated for a time whether to choose Oxford or Cambridge or London, and finally settled on London. They were fortunate in finding a two-roomed flat in the Islington district not quite beyond their means, and there they began their new life together.

The arrangement worked well. It was agreed that housekeeping chores be shared between them — and if in practice Vi was doing a good deal more cooking and cleaning than Leonard, that was because the institutions he needed to visit were more numerous and more scattered than hers. The British Library for the most part, occasionally the Warburg Institute, were sufficient for her outside needs, while the generous lending facilities of the

London Library enabled much of her research to be pursued at home.

Not that they spent all their time working. Though neither played an instrument, they were both fond of classical music, and they made good use of the rich variety of orchestral and chamber concerts Londoners are privileged to enjoy. Nor were they indifferent to the theatre. Moreover they both liked walking, and a fine day could still tempt them to a day in the country, even though it now meant a journey by coach or train to get there. Social life was bounded at first by two or three friends who lived not too far away and later by a small circle consisting of these and a few others introduced by them.

As to anything wider, neither was much interested in politics. Once, moved by a vague sense of duty rather than by inclination, they went to a party meeting and heard the address of a visiting celebrity. But that was all. Neither had ever experienced a world unblessed by television, and their shared attitude to politics may be described as a confused impression, rather than a considered judgment, that parliament was a place where almost anything proposed by the party in office was sure to be immediately denounced by the opposition, as "squalid" or "obscene", and that politicians were an alien race more concerned with their "image" than with the practical results of anything they might say.

Two years passed quickly and smoothly, and the time arrived when they both took their degrees and academic life was at an end, unless one or both of them should adopt it as a means of livelihood. What next? It was a question they had decided in advance after much intervening discussion. He would apply for a University appointment and be the breadwinner. It was not disputed that Vi was equally capable of earning in that way nor tacitly assumed that the fact of her sex made it less appropriate for her to do so. It was just that the kind of work she wanted to do was not likely to bring in any money, at least until some considerable time had elapsed, and that in any case it could best be done at home.

You could say in general that Vi had literary ambitions, or that she thought of carrying much further the research in her thesis, or that she was toying with the idea of expanding and turning it into a book, or that she contemplated writing a book along the lines it suggested. She herself hardly knew which. Her character was less crystallised than was Leonard's, who saw his way ahead in clear outlines. If her self-knowledge was deeper than his, there was plenty there besides literary ambition, of which she as yet knew little.

After one or two failures Leonard succeeded in obtaining a satisfactory tutorial appointment at a university in the Midlands, with prospects, if all went well, of a research fellowship later on; and they said good-bye to London without much regret. It meant a big change in their way of life. With the help of a mortgage they could now afford a small semi-detached house in a suburb of the university town. Country walks were more accessible, though now, save during vacations, they were limited to weekends. Old friends were lost sight of. New ones began to materialise from among the faculty and their wives. And now they decided to get married themselves. It was a change in their relationship of which they felt less conscious than they did of most other changes in their lives. As with many, or perhaps most, of their contemporaries, since it did not mark the beginning of cohabitation, the actual event was something they drifted into rather than celebrated. And when it was over, and they had returned from the Registry Office, they had only to confirm a decision long since agreed on to defer the arrival of a child or children, "at all events for the present".

Again the arrangement worked well enough. They were not merely regarded by their friends and acquaintances — which is common enough — as a happy couple; but — which is less common — they actually were one. Of course there were passing clouds — mainly as yet low on the horizon — clouds which perhaps originated in the very fact that they had so much in common. Both were enthusiastically involved in their work, and in both cases that work lay in the direction of enquiry into the past life and behaviour of mankind. Here the only difference was that Vi was looking for fresh interpretations of ancient art and literature, whereas Leonard's field was the remoter, pre-documentary past of the human race.

Leonard was the more extrovert of the two. It was natural to him to grow more and more interested in the *method* of his science, and its increasingly complex development, less so in any speculative inferences to be drawn from its results. He was happiest on a 'dig', when he was visiting — or with luck participating in — the excavation of a new site. He felt nearest to paradise when he was surrounded by careful measurements and reverently removed, scrupulously cleaned, and neatly wrapped and docketed fragments. Not that he degenerated into a mere 'research beetle' or *never* dreamed up a wondering picture of the daily lives of those vanished palaeolithic or even eolithic men who were his chosen quarry. Chosen, it must be said, after a good deal of hesitation and some tentative sallies into later periods — including even the Iron Age, to which he had felt drawn for a time after that memorable walk on Fraxon Down. In short, Leonard was a good professional archaeologist with the honourable ambition to become a better one.

Vi on the other hand, when she turned her mind to it, was less intrigued by what those primitive men might have been doing than by what they might have been feeling and thinking. But this is to look ahead. For the present it was her own field that held all her interest, a field whose data were so different from the ones Leonard had to deal with — not grubby bits of stone that might or might not be artifacts, and so forth, but books, some well known and some conspicuously ignored, illuminated manuscripts, stained glass windows and statuary, and the cathedrals that housed them. She had, incidentally, some small talent for sketching and she soon acquired the habit of re-drawing in her notebooks one or two medieval scenes and figures — reproduced in a library book from their original glass or parchment — which for some reason particularly appealed to her. If because of their preoccupation with their own concerns neither was disposed to enter at all deeply into those of the other, there was one thing on which they were both agreed and frequently commented. There was too much 'secondary material'. The accelerating expansion of recorded 'culture' since the war, the university explosion in Europe and America and so forth — all these might be very fine things, but it had meant too many books, too many articles, dissertations, monographs, etc., pouring monthly from the presses. And now the advent of the computer looked to double both the quantity of material and the speed at which it accumulated. No one nowadays could hope to keep up with recent and contemporary literature on his subject and everyone spent far too much valuable time trying to do so.

Navigating — or at all events remaining afloat — in the plethora was a somewhat less hopeless task for Vi than for Leonard. This was because she had a focused interest to pursue. Her sights were fixed, as it were, on a particular point in the literary horizon, namely the nature and significance of allegory. This operated as a selector in somewhat the same way that a stick inserted into an amorphous and potentially crystalline mass will produce and gather a limited cluster of crystals round itself. Nor was it only with proliferating secondary material that it helped; it mitigated that despairing reflection known to many a student gazing round the well-filled shelves of a large library: how many of these books can I ever hope to read? What is the use of it all?

Like Leonard, Vi had been tempted to other options before selecting her field. The strongest of these was the Romantic period. And it was the effect on her speculative disposition of something she found there that had finally sent her back to the Middle Ages. Many of the

Romantics Symbolism good, allegory bad

Romantics, and still more of their later exponents, held strong views on the inferior status of allegory as a literary genre. Symbolism — and its earlier subconscious equivalent, myth — was a good thing because it embodied "creative imagination". Allegory, especially with its penchant for personification, was a bad thing, because it was lifeless, abstract thought disguising itself as imagination. This seemed taken for granted by everybody in that field who was anybody, and Vi had accepted it wholeheartedly as the truth of the matter. Only later did the pebble of doubt drop into the pool of conviction and disturb its surface. Her mind went back to her undergraduate days and her own encounters with allegory in the poets, not only *Pearl* or *The Faerie Queen*, but even such interminably and aggressively allegorical monsters as *The Romaunt of the Rose*. Whatever her professors and her textbooks might say, she had been intrigued by it, had positively revelled in it. Not being a conceited young woman, her first reaction had been one of something like guilt. Something must be wrong with her if she enjoyed stuff that all the best people found insipid. But not being a timid young woman, further reflection led her to decide it was no use pretending she didn't like what she did like. If, when she kept encountering the Seven Liberal Arts, for example, she began to feel about them, not a revulsion from such arid personifications, but something more like the sort of affection novel-readers come to feel for the characters in Jane Austen or Anthony Trollope, well, so be it! However wrong-headed it might be, she must follow her own taste and see where it led her.

And of course it led her into unexpected places, some of them places that no longer had anything to do with allegory — unless on your way back into the past you recognised them as a seed-bed from which not allegory alone but much else had proceeded. For example, it was from the *Psychomachia* of Prudentius that she was led on to explore the whole bizarre and tangled history of *amour courtois*, that old troubadour syndrome (so much deeper rooted than Keats's "Dance and Provençal Song and sunburnt mirth"), and the mental world of the *Fedeli d'amore* revealed in Dante's *Vita Nuova*. On the other hand, it was from the one or two little-known contemporary critics who were beginning to oppose the conventional distaste for it, and for whose support she was so grateful, that she acquired the habit of seeing in medieval allegory not only the personification of intellectual abstractions but also the legitimate offspring of ancient and vigorous myth.

Here was yet another lead. Myth — and all that the word implies of another kind of consciousness from today's — so many outside the academic world, and a few within it, were on their way to abandoning the nineteenth-century James Frazer view of it. If the myths were indeed simply invented stories clothing ideas and beliefs, how did they differ from allegories? Why was their vitality so self-evident? The tenor of such speculations led her inevitably to Jungian psychology, and for a time she was satisfied with the Unconscious and its 'primordial images' as a sufficient answer. But only for a time. Primordial images — archetypes — where did *they* come from? According to

Jung, in one of his moods, they appear in our dreams today because they are "psychic residua of numberless experiences of the same type". But how had *those* experiences begun to appear in the dreams or otherwise of the primitive human beings, whose scanty vestiges were her husband's happy hunting-ground? Presumably they had not *got* any residue. Well, the answer was of course that they had been "projected" on the outside world by an inside world called consciousness, when it was awake, and "the unconscious" when it was asleep or dreaming. But this, to her industriously prying mind, sounded suspiciously like the old "animism" of the anthropologists and not all that different from Frazer and invented fictions. If it was true, it seemed to imply that myth had begun life as allegory — allegory as understood and pooh-poohed by the Romantics. Whereas Vi was feeling more and more certain that allegory had descended lineally from myth.

One thing was certain. Her own interests had now gone far beyond anything she had put in her doctoral Thesis. If she was to write anything, it would have to be a book or a monograph, for which the Thesis would be of little use. But she was not certain enough of anything to start on a book. That might come later. She little knew how different what she would in the end come to write was to be from the sort of thing she was vaguely envisaging.

CHAPTER III

THESE ADVENTURES OF the mind, important to her as they were, were something she found impossible to share with Leo. She made one or two attempts at the early stage when it was still all speculation and no conviction, but his response was, to say the least of it, discouraging. Whatever he said or tried to say, he obviously could not see what there was to be excited about. She felt a little wounded and relapsed into silence. The wound healed quickly enough, but she continued to feel distressed by the communication gap that had opened between them, and later on she made one more attempt to bridge it. Among his archaeological books there was one meant to be a general introduction to the subject, lavishly illustrated, and covering all periods from the Stone Age to the Iron Age. One evening Vi looked up from a casual perusal of it. She had it open at a plate showing some of the wall-paintings in the caves of the Pyrenees and the Dordogne.

"Can I interrupt you?"

"Yes, of course."

"How does archaeology account for the fact that palaeolithic man was so much better an artist than neolithic man?"

Leo had first to wrench his mind away from the monograph he had been reading. When he had done so, he said patiently, "I don't know that it does account for it. Does it matter?"

She began trying to explain why it mattered — to her anyway. The result was an unsatisfactory conversation in

which she had a great deal more to say than he had.
Indeed it became clear almost from the beginning that he
would be glad to bring it to an end. Her idea was to raise
the question of the inner world, the type of consciousness,
enjoyed by Stone Age men and to suggest that it might be
more important, a more fruitful field for research, than
their outward circumstances.

"You mean their motives? I imagine they were too busy
hunting and fighting and keeping warm and keeping
themselves alive to have much time for an inner life!"

Discouraged, she persisted a little longer. That was
what one might have thought, she said, but — and she
raised again the question of Stone Age man's artistic
abilities, and the fact that they had apparently declined
instead of improving, in accordance with the law of
progressive evolution.

But Leo was not to be drawn. "We just don't know why
it was," he said. "And we probably never shall know.
There's no way of finding out." And he went back to his
reading.

The effect of the conversation on Vi was out of all
proportion to its ostensible content. An obscure stirring
of the spirit beneath the everyday life of the soul, so far
beneath it that it is a secret stirring, is very vulnerable.
Any attempt to disclose the secret by communicating its
nature to another mind must reckon with a snail-horn
sensitivity of the soul. A repulse — and mere
incomprehension will count as such — can be like a blow
in the face. It is as if you had spent years and years writing
an epic poem, and, when at last it was published, the

world had simply laughed at it or brushed it aside. Vi never tried again.

The effect of her failure was not traumatic. Leo knew nothing about it, and it could not be said that Vi was unhappy. The two went on living comfortably together. But at some level or other Vi was troubled. If you had asked her, she might have said there was nothing amiss; yet she knew in her heart that their intimacy had been damaged. It was the more unfortunate that another more serious and more overt rift was threatening between them.

Vi, as has been said, was not 'politicized'. She was not exceptionally aware of social inequalities or concerned with attempts to improve them by legislation or otherwise. On the other hand she was very sensitively aware of much that was going on in the world around her, to which politics was irrelevant. Call it the technological explosion, or, less sensationally, the accelerating pace at which technology was interfering with the given life and processes of nature. It was at about this time that such an awareness was beginning to spread among the general public, after having long been confined to a few eccentric individuals and movements. Barely a week passed without some television programme calculated to awaken and even to alarm by its disclosures. If the problem of disposing of nuclear waste had first sounded the alarm, concern over much else quite unconnected with that, had soon taken over. Viewers were being shown glimpses not only of reckless deforestation all over Europe, but also of an increasingly systematic commercial clearing of tropical jungles that must leave them, after a year or two of cash crops, a lifeless desert of soil erosion and infertility for the rest of time. People were being made to think of the long-term effects of all this on the whole future of mankind; and even of the earth itself. 'Pollution' was becoming almost a vogue word, as the scale on which it was taking place became more and more apparent.

What was new was not the process itself. For decades past the waters of Lake Erie, for example, had been too contaminated to support any aquatic life, and the well-informed tourist who stood contemplating Niagara Falls, knew he was looking at what was in effect a discharge of sewage. What *was* new was, first, the pace at which pollution was accelerating and, secondly, the growing general awareness of it. Nor was the scourge of pollution confined to waste products and the modern practice of attempting to dispose of them otherwise than by recycling them through the life-forms in nature herself. Much, or most, of the packaged foodstuffs in a supermarket were tainted with chemical preservatives and flavouring additives, whose immediate effects might be shown by tests to be harmless, but whose long-term effects on health and stamina would not be known until well into the future. Marketing skills had been growing at the speed of Jack's beanstalk. An orange or a strawberry preserve or a beef extract might contain no actual orange or strawberry or beef at all. And even the natural product itself was no longer natural. Factory farming, hormone fattening and genetic engineering were seeing to that.

Television, although not very prominently, was starting to bring all this to light. People were actually seeing what they had hitherto only heard of, if that: rows and rows of hens kept alive by antibiotics and insecticides and prevented from pecking each other to death only by diurnal tranquillisers; similar rows of boxed-in calves or bullocks that never saw a green field or the open sky between birth and slaughter. And there was more to the same effect, while the dismayed onlooker, who was driven to take refuge in a strictly vegetarian diet, might make what he could of the acres of farmland he was shown, converted into virtual prairie for the convenience of cultivation by biennial visits from a hired tractor, and sprayed assiduously with herbicides and pesticides in between.

Vi was among those on whom all this left a deep impression, or something more like a deep wound. Yet when she tried to share her concern with Leo, she failed again; and this time the failure bit deeper into her soul. Of course he understood what she was saying, but he could not grasp how deeply she felt it.

"What's the use of brooding over it?" was his final response. "We can't *do* anything."

That was an answer she never forgot, as she nevertheless continued to brood. Not on any one in particular of all the symptoms that were being brought to light. It was the total of them. They were witnessing before their very eyes what could only be called — and the metaphor arose naturally in her mind and stayed there — the *rape* of nature, the rape of the very earth itself. And she had been told they could not do anything! The slight rift between them, which had opened on other grounds, was growing wider, and its effects began to reach the surface in minor irritations, abruptnesses of response or behaviour that had formerly been foreign to them, as well as in other little things too slight to record but not too slight to hurt a little at the time.

And what of Leonard? It must not be thought that he failed to notice them or to feel unhappy. If he lacked the self-knowledge that might have enabled him to analyse them, he by no means lacked the sensitivity that is vulnerable to an almost imperceptible rebuff. Indeed he actually *suffered* more than his wife. Some Frenchman or other, with his national penchant for carrying cool analysis to the point of cynicism, has remarked that, in a love affair, there is always a lover and a beloved; one of the two always loves rather more, and is loved rather less than the other. Whether that is generally true or not, it was true of 'this ever diverse pair'. Poor Leonard, without his knowing it, had always been the more passionate, the more devoted of the two. He was correspondingly the more hurt by the little withdrawals that any sort of rift entails. But he was quite incapable of tabulating or even perhaps of naming them mentally, still more so of tracing them to their source or bringing them to the surface by articulating them.

Vi could have done that, but she shrank from it, fearing where it might lead. So both of them suffered in silence. If Leonard felt it more, Vi was the one who thought about it. The unease, the uncertainty even, as to precisely what 'it' was, kept coming back into her mind at any time when it was not preoccupied, and sometimes even when it was. Inevitably her attempts to fathom the gulf between them

linked themselves with the convictions and still more with
the speculations arising from her studies. She tried to get
them to throw some light on it. She even went so far on
one occasion as to ask herself whether she had anything
to learn from the attitude to the sexual relation that
transpired through the *amour courtois* tradition. Or was
that all over and done with long ago? A line from one of
Charles Williams' poems slid into her mind: "The lifting
of her eyelash is my Lord". Was she a lady? Was she
beautiful? Should she — but this avenue led swiftly to a
big laugh at the momentary glimpse it called up of Leo
adoring her on his knees. But then — for Vi knew much
more about herself than she knew about Leo — even the
laugh was called in question, as she found herself recalling
certain things that had puzzled her at the time after their
moments of high passion — an involuntary gesture, a look
on his face, a tiny nuance of behaviour that she had soon
forgotten. Might things have gone better if they had
followed the out-of-date rule of postponing physical
intercourse until after marriage? Perhaps. Perhaps not.
Perhaps things might have gone worse. She had no idea.
Her introspection led nowhere. It was all reflection and
no conclusions.

CHAPTER IV

THUS THINGS GREW worse rather than better. Instead of being healed, as it might possibly have been if they had confronted it together, the rift was imperceptibly widening. One result, in Vi's case, was her throwing herself into her studies, not perhaps with more energy, but certainly with more warmth than heretofore. Thoughts about the kind of book she might write, though still vague enough, were somehow less shadowy. Another result, which suited them both, was that they spent less time alone together and more with friends or acquaintances. Although Vi was not a member of the university, she had been introduced to one or two of the faculty, mainly in the Department of English, though the one with whom she felt most *en rapport* taught History of Art. Their fields overlapped because iconography cannot avoid overlapping with iconology.

John Herapath had recently published an article with much to interest her. A sentence or two, such as "Allegory is related to myth as heraldry to painting", stayed in her mind and made her think. It was not long before they were meeting regularly. He introduced her to unsuspected depths in the medieval and pre-medieval concept, or rather assumption, of biblical typology. She disclosed her speculations on and difficulties with the Jungian "archetype" and its bearing on the supposed consciousness of pre-documentary man. She was pleased to confirm her suspicion that the theory of "projection" made nonsense. The imagery and symbolism embodied in the perdurable myths, if they were projected at all, were projected or rather implanted in man's mind from the world around him, from nature herself and what lay behind nature. This was something for her to take away and ruminate on, and she did not fail to do so.

Herapath was acquainted with her husband, though only superficially. Vi had mentioned her unsatisfactory attempt at a discussion with Leo that might relate his archaeological bent to her aesthetic and psychological one. Now the idea occurred to her of trying again, this time with Herapath's help. Leo agreed amicably enough to her suggestion of asking him to dinner, and a few days later brought Herapath back with him from the university in the evening. Vi was not a bad cook and she had taken extra trouble to provide an appetising meal with tasty garnishings and a suitable wine. Table talk accordingly was quite lively, centring mainly on the university, its shortcomings and prospects, with ramifications into the amusing foibles of certain members of the staff. Only after dinner, as they sat over their coffee, did conversation begin to flag. Leo's disposition was on the whole taciturn; Vi was nervous; and Herapath, who had guessed her motive in arranging the meeting, was chiefly anxious to say the right thing, whatever it might be. A silence ensued which made him feel called on to start the ball rolling, Vi being apparently unwilling to do so.

"Vi tells me," he began, and it was perhaps not the most tactful start he could have chosen, "that archaeologists are only interested in the living conditions of the people whose remains they excavate, not in their minds."

"Hardly," said Leo. "We are interested in everything to do with them."

"You did say, you know," said Vi slowly, "that we had no means of knowing what was going on in their minds."

"Yes, but you were talking about art, or something of the sort. We infer from what they did their motives for doing it."

"Yes, I see that," put in Herapath, "but mightn't a good many alternative inferences be possible?"

"No, I don't think so. We know what our own motives would have been for doing the same thing."

"Drawing pictures on cave walls, for instance?"

"Oh, there are various theories about that — hunting rituals, control by magic, and so forth."

"I think Vi's problem," said Herapath, "is that that wouldn't explain the *quality* of some of the drawings, their positive excellence."

"Oh well, that goes rather beyond archaeology. Archaeology depends on *evidence*."

There followed a few moments of silence. After some hesitation, Herapath decided to break it.

"I think," he said, "Vi is also interested in the origin of myths. So am I, as a matter of fact. A good deal seems to have been going on in those minds besides the best way of dealing with the problem of survival. Was it G.K. Chesterton, or someone else, who said: 'The one thing we know about primitive man is that he was not primitive'?"

"You must go to the anthropologists for all that," said Leo. "It's outside my domain, I'm afraid." And there was something in his tone that made his visitor feel the subject had better be dropped. It was getting fairly late and, with an appropriate excuse and the customary thanks to them both, he left not long afterwards.

When Leo came back from seeing Herapath out, Vi asked him if he had enjoyed the visit. Leo thought he seemed a pleasant fellow and said yes, he had enjoyed it. She hoped he would say something more, but it seemed he had nothing more to say. This did not surprise her, since hoping he would say something when he didn't was a thing she had become accustomed to. But a slight something in his manner made her look at him rather closely and conclude that he had guessed her motive for inviting Herapath and was in a manner reflecting on it. She decided not to repeat the experiment, or at all events not for some time.

But the fact that Herapath had been in her home helped to strengthen the atmosphere of sympathy between the two; she began seeing him rather more often, and their talks grew longer and more probing, that is to say more likely to touch on first principles. Herapath was a thoughtful and well-read man. So when Vi went back on one occasion to the topic of the supposed origin of myths in "projection", and told him she still found his view puzzling, he hesitated for a while, as if deliberating whether or not to take a plunge, and then said:

"I'm not surprised. You find it difficult, as everyone does — as no doubt Jung did with his background in the Victorian scientific paradigm — to imagine the traffic, so to speak, between nature and mind having gone in the *opposite* direction."

"Opposite?"

"I mean, instead of the mind inventing images and plastering them on the face of nature, to imagine nature giving her substance to mind."

"That's difficult — her *substance*?"

Again he hesitated. "The trouble is," he said at last, "that there *is* a sort of metaphorical truth in the 'projection' way of putting it. It's all right to say a tree 'thrusts its roots into the earth', as long as that doesn't make you forget that the roots were there from the beginning, and the tree draws all its strength from them. You have to think of an immaterial nature made of active forces — *natura naturans*, if you like — bringing to birth on the one hand what we call the outside world and, along with it, on the other, not only the human physical brain and so on, but also human imagination."

Vi did not look very hopeful.

"But you can only do that," he went on "if you can stop imagining the mind as somehow *inside* the brain. And it's not easy. We all do it. I don't mean we all *think* that way. Quite a few people see through the fallacy intellectually, but they still go on imagining mind and thought in those terms."

Vi was silent. And so was he for some moments. Then he got up and took down a book.

"I found the other way of seeing things very well put by Hegel in a single sentence, rather a long one, but the point is that it is aimed at the imagination as well as the reason. Shall I read it to you?" She nodded, and he opened the book.

As the lightning sleeps in the dewdrop [he read], so in the simple and transparent unity of self-consciousness there is held in equilibrium that vital antagonism of opposites, which, as the opposition of thought and things, of mind and matter, of spirit and nature, seems to rend the world asunder.

He shut the book and looked up at her. But she was still not with him.

"Antagonism of opposites," she said, "between spirit and nature. Yes, of course, but – "

"Oppositeness is not the same as otherness," he interrupted. "A point in a circle is opposite to another point in the same circle. Heads and tails are opposite sides of the same coin, not two different coins."

Vi was not one to pretend she understood when she didn't, or that she "saw" when she did not. She remained silent.

"Do you see the bearing of it on what we have been talking about?"

"Well – " She stopped short. And they both laughed.

Next time they met, however, she was able to tell him she thought perhaps she *was* beginning to see. "It helps me a good deal," she said. For instance, I think I understand better some of the things you were saying about *Genius* (I mean medieval *Genius*) the other day, yes, and about *Natura* seen as a goddess — *felt* as a goddess rather. *Seen* by your artists, felt by my poets."

Herapath was pleased. He decided to lay on the table a card he had purposely been withholding.

"Let's leave aside *Genius* and *Natura* and *medium aevum*

and all that for the moment," he said. "You remember your husband saying there was no way of finding out the mental processes of Stone Age man? Well, he was wrong. There is a way — and not only of Stone Age man, but much farther back than that." He paused, and she looked a question at him.

"I don't suppose you have ever heard of the Akashic Record?" he asked, and she shook her head. He went on then to speak at some length. For some time past, he said, he had been studying the work of Rudolf Steiner. She had heard of him, of course, but knew little about him. He enlightened her with a brief description of the Anthroposophical Movement and its activities before coming back to the point at issue. "So you see, the contention is," he concluded, "that just as, if you want to know about the physical world and its past, you have to investigate whatever your senses can find, if you want to investigate the mental and spiritual past, you have to investigate whatever your mind can find — *find*, not just fancy. And the difference is that whereas sense-perceptible objects decay and vanish with the passing of time, mental experiences and events do not. They persist in a kind of Cosmic Memory and are accessible to some who know how to explore it."

"But *how* do they explore it?"

"It would take too long to go into that. There is a theory of knowledge. I find it convincing. But it would take too long to go into. We can get a bare glimpse of it, if we think of Imagination (with a capital 'I') supplementing inference in the process of cognition.

I want to assume for the moment that it is valid, that that alternative method of research is possible, and in particular that Steiner himself pursued it successfully." And with that Herapath reverted to the old question of the origin of myth and its "archetypes".

Vi was a little shaken. But she had confidence in Herapath, had in fact been impressed both by his common sense and by his sincerity ever since their first meeting. In the upshot she decided of her own accord — he made no such suggestion — to study Steiner, or some of him, for herself.

There is no need to go into what she found: her delight in some parts of it, her doubts and bewilderment in others. Perhaps she would have dropped it had she not been so deeply impressed by his treatment of one or two particular Greek myths. For example the picture he left with her of the birth of Medusa, of immaterial forces — or were they Beings? — gradually bringing into visible manifestation, on the one hand the convolutions of the brain and on the other the mental image (image or Imagination?) of the writhing snakes that were the Gorgon's hair — the Gorgon who turned to stone whatever she looked on, as the brain (so Wordsworth had taught her) "murders to dissect."

But then there was so much more, a whole new world that somehow embraced the familiar one and in doing so illuminated and explained it. What was most noticeable for her, however, was that she kept meeting ideas and beings that were familiar to her, not as parts of the real world but as parts of her scholarship: the planetary spheres, the nine Hierarchies of angelic beings named by Dionysius the

Areopagite, the four elements and their lively interpenetration. She had not been uninterested in them, far from it, but she had been interested in them as literary phenomena. Now she had to get used to finding them spoken of, not as material for a dissertation or, at the most, interesting historical fantasies, but as pawns on an elaborate chessboard of exposition, no less substantial than such historically vouched pawns as Plato or Alain of Lille or Wolfram von Eschenbach. Hesitantly she kept in touch with Herapath, took his suggestions as to what she might select from the vast body of anthroposophical literature, and sometimes offered her comments, including some sceptical ones. To these his usual response was: "All that matters is whether you are interested or not;" but on one occasion, when she protested that she was being asked to "put the clock back", he reminded her of things they had said when talking of Jung about "the traffic between mind and nature". The traffic *had* begun to go the opposite way by the time Steiner taught, he said. No longer from nature to mind, as in the past, no longer in the direction Jung had tried to reverse with his purely subjective concept of the Unconscious, but *really* from mind to nature — from the conscious mind to nature. And then he skilfully turned her own guns on her. Had she not herself detected the change of direction actually taking place — in the transition from myth to allegory?

It may sometimes happen that a single brief thought, whether it has been read in a book or heard in conversation, or whether it has simply arisen in the mind apparently of its own accord, acts as a catalyst. Or perhaps the shaking of a kaleidoscope is a better image. A few moments' reflection on it and the whole series is rearranged, some parts separated, others fused. In Vi's case it was fusion that predominated, for this remark of Herapath's actually united in her mind the two subjects with which she had long been separately obsessed. Two dimly apprehended ideas had become one clearly understood one, and she felt enlightened as she had never been enlightened before. The first result was a less than sober enthusiasm. The new light must be strong enough to solve all problems. It *must* be possible to share some of it with Leonard, to make him understand something of what was working in her.

"Leo," she said on the following evening, breaking the silence in which they stood washing up the supper things, "I have been talking to Herapath again."

"Oh yes?"

She paused while she held up to the light a glass tumbler she had been wiping. "He threw a lot of light on things for me."

"He certainly has his own ideas."

Vi suppressed a pusillanimous impulse to drop the subject. She pushed herself to keep the ball rolling. "You remember that evening he came to dinner? I wished afterwards that we had gone on a bit longer."

"Gone on a bit longer?"

"I mean, with the subject we started on. About archaeology. I didn't really try to make clear what I had in mind. It wasn't just particular theories about the — the mental processes of Stone Age man and so forth. It's the whole question of the relation of human consciousness and its physical environment."

She paused and Leonard made no comment.

"Has it changed, and in what way has it changed? That's what I was trying to get at."

The washing up was concluded. Leo proceeded with the necessary swilling down of the draining board and they returned in silence to the living room. As they settled into their chairs Vi cast about rather desperately for some way of arresting the threatened relapse into silence. An idea came to her.

"You remember," she asked, "that last year at Cartishall, when we used to visit Harry Coppard?" And, without waiting for a reply: "We talked a good deal about him. And we also used to talk more about our work. I remember — perhaps it was a little earlier on — trying to explain why I was so interested in the relation between myth and allegory."

She paused, not as if waiting for an answer, but reflectively. Then, not reproachfully, but with a touch of wistful humour, she said: "You weren't very forthcoming."

Absorbed now in her reflection, and protected by it from any repulse his silence might imply, she soon added; "The point is that it's the same thing."

"I don't follow. What is the same thing?"

"Can't you see? The *change of direction* — our private consciousness, all subjective experience, given to us long ago by Nature, drawn from the life of Nature like water from a sponge. That was what the myths were doing, and at the end the sponge was left dry and falling to pieces. And that now we have to give back what we have got; that was what allegory was beginning to do, only it didn't know it. But it's also what Harry is trying to do in his very practical way."

Leo got up and began to walk to and fro. He was chiefly conscious of an anxiety not to hurt by snubbing. But it was also no use pretending.

"I'm afraid I *can't* see it," he said. "Of course what men *do* — and what they have done — to nature matters. But I don't believe nature cares twopence what we *think* about it. Nature is governed by laws we didn't make and can't alter." He stopped walking and added: "All I *can* see is that you've got hold of a theory that means a lot to you. It looks as if we shall have to leave it at that."

Poor Virginia! She had made such an effort, and its nil return was so final. Leo sat down and took up a book. She did the same and pretended to read, while she went on thinking. Sharing then was out. So where did she stand? The enlightenment, she found, was there as firm as ever; but the accompanying warmth of enthusiasm had gone away.

She made no further attempt to interest Leo in what was going on in her, feeling certain now that it would be useless. And so, as time went on, she became aware of a painful cleft, or contradiction. The clearer she grew about the meaning of life in general, the darker grew the horizon of her personal life, the tougher its problems. She was both happier and unhappier, more and more at a loss what to do in the one direction, less and less so in the other. And a second long conversation with Herapath soon came to emphasize the cleft.

She had begun it by suggesting that she should
recapitulate, as from student to teacher, the substance of
the last one:

"As I understand it, the Spirit first created mankind, and
the earth, and then *entered* them. But then it retired from
the natural world in order to constitute man a free
autonomous being. It then became his task to give back
to the earth the spiritual life with which he had been
endowed."

Herapath's response was unexpected. "And this re-
union," he added slowly, "is the true meaning of the words
knowledge and *science*." Then his manner changed. It was
as if he shook himself; he started talking quickly, you could
almost say *testily*: "But it's all too dry and abstract. If you
want to *realise* it, I advise you to read some of the things
that Steiner taught concerning the archangel Michael —
or better say, the Being identified by some ancient
Hebrews as Michael, but for whom others have found
other names." And he mentioned in particular one of a
series of lectures on the seasons of the year, the one on
Michaelmas.

Vi did more than read it. She meditated on it. It left
her mind impressed with two seminal pictures —
Imaginations, certainly, but real ones. The first was none
other than the immemorial one of Michael subduing the
Dragon, but with the Dragon-figure symbolizing the
Adversary himself, to whom the Lecturer gave the name
of Ahriman. The second, in more indefinite outlines, was
of the metal, Iron, seen in two opposite aspects — one of
them being iron in industrial and commercial use and the

other the spiritual iron to be found both in human will and
— here was the surprise — in the uncontaminated
meteoric showers that from time to time reach earth from
outer space. In this connection the August Perseids (and
Vi was reminded of the shower of gold that begot the
mythical Perseus) were specifically mentioned, and it was
perhaps this picture that took firmest hold of her
imagination. And yet … "Can you really accept – " she
had begun; but Herapath had nodded an interruption:

"The meteor showers? Yes. The — what is it the meek
Dualists call it? — the 'objective correlative' to the iron in
human blood."

The Lecturer had concluded with something like an
exhortation, strophically emphasised, to the human race.
"You subdue it to your service," they were warned, "and
in doing so you bring out its material value. But it will only
bring healing when your eyes are opened to the majestic
spiritual vigour it embodies". It was at this point in her
tour of mental exploration that not only Vi's imagination
but her memory received a jolt. Quite suddenly she was
taken back to a month in her past life she had almost
forgotten, and it was as if "taken back" was more than a
metaphor. For a few minutes it was as though an operation
had been performed on her brain, eliminating the whole
of her subsequent life. For a few minutes she *was* the Vi
of those old days. Harry Coppard, his cottage and his
acorns, sitting there talking to him, the trees, the long
summer day's walk, Eager Spring — they were all there
still, it seemed. The vividness of recollection, as it faded,
was succeeded by something like a rush of compunction.

It was not only outward impressions that she had let go. Those long talks with Harry. For the last few months she had almost lost sight of that repugnance to the rape of the earth which he had evoked or awakened in her, though up to then it had been growing stronger rather than weaker. Well, it was to be so no longer. From now on her two preoccupations — or were they obsessions? — were fused, for good or ill, with one another.

CHAPTER V

THE NEXT TIME she met Herapath, she asked him some questions about the established followers of this man Steiner. Herapath was not, it appeared, a member of any Society, but he occasionally attended meetings of Anthroposophists that were held in the neighbouring town. She asked him whether they were doing anything to counter some of those technological assaults that she was in the habit of classing together as the 'rape of the earth'. He told her as much as he knew about Bio-Dynamic Farming, founded on Steiner's revelations, very much aware of the assaults and determined to avoid them. But that was not quite what she meant.

"Are they doing anything to stop what is going on *now*?" she asked him. And he could only say that, as far as he knew, they were not.

"How can they see so clearly what is going wrong, and do nothing about it?"

"If you mean protests, demonstrations — that sort of thing — they don't do anything like it as a Society. I don't know what some of them may do as individuals." He went on to murmur something about future incarnations, and that they felt they were preparing themselves for worse things to come. She said nothing. But she was not satisfied. Their apparent impotence, or lack of inclination, to meet what she saw as the immediate crisis, had kept her from involvement with such movements as the Soil Association or the Men of the Trees. All very well to attack the disease rather than the symptoms, but if the symptoms have become disastrous, their treatment must come first.

Now she was inwardly, was perpetually, disturbed to an extent she had never known before. Leo noticed the change in her, the longer silences and the abstracted look, and it troubled him. But he felt too cut off from her to ask if anything was the matter. Round and round went the thoughts in her head, as she went to and fro about the house. Round and round, not so much like the wheels in a machine, more like the roots in a flower pot, thinly round and round and over and under each other, because they are trying to swell within a pot that is too tight for them. Iron! Had it all begun with the Iron Age? And backward bent the thoughts, curling and creeping round each other in their own world. The Age when the Change of Direction was happening, when the 'given' spirit was drying out of words and images and minds, and beginning in consequence to be driven out of the world of things — the denaturing of Nature that had begun with the scientific revolution. Back again, now, to herself, Virginia Brook, and the world of today — the Plastics Age — the world she was living in, the world she was in a measure responsible for. What was she to *do*?

In the end she felt it was wrong to hide the pressure from Leo any longer. It was difficult to broach the subject, but she managed somehow. She recalled to him the last time they had spoken about it. "You said we can't *do* anything. Harry Coppard is doing something — has been for years."

"Yes, but we're not Harry Coppard."

"He is doing what his particular situation suggested. It

may not be much but it's something. We ought to be able to do something *our* situation suggests."

"And what is that?"

"*I* don't know," she said angrily. "I feel we can't just stand looking on any longer." And she turned away.

Did all she had been trying to say sound sensational and silly in his ears? If so he did not show it. He did not share her feeling, but simply to have been living in the same house with her for the last few weeks was evidence enough of its force. He at least *looked* sympathetic, and for a time there was more harmony between them. This made it easier for her to tell him of a decision she came to a little later.

In their part of the country there were no conspicuously grievous technological assaults to object to — no threatening nuclear or chemical plant, no more than the usual spraying with fertilizers and pesticides. But she saw a newspaper notice of a meeting called by the local group of one of several ecological or environmental organisations that had come into being during the last few years, and she attended it. When she got home, she told her husband she had joined it. He looked a little surprised, perhaps a little uneasy, but he raised no objection. There was indeed not much to object to. Vi herself felt how remote it all was from the strident "Green" movement whose sometimes aggressive activities were often in the news in England, and which in some European countries were growing up into political parties. There was little that these Earth-lovers, as they named themselves, could do in this part of the world, beyond keeping a sharp eye on straw-burning,

excessive spraying, and the unlawful obliteration of
footpaths. So even though she took an active part in a not
very active Association, and was even made a member of
its Committee, it did little to relax the internal pressure.
It was not the sort of pressure she could reveal to
Herapath. He was not that kind of man. Art and its
history were all in all to him, as Archaeology was all in all
to Leo. If there was a crisis in human affairs, for Herapath
the issue at stake was whether Art was in terminal decline,
or whether the birth of a new inspiration was in prospect.

Another problem round which some of her thoughts
had started to revolve was one she did at first think she
might open to him, since it as nearer to their common
field; but for various reasons she refrained from doing so.
Round and round they still went, the uncertain thoughts,
driven by their frustrated impulse to sprout. This time the
Romaunt of the Rose, *Amour Courtois* and the *Fedeli d'Amore*
joined in the circus: Earth-lovers! Did they really love it?
What was the meaning of love? There was plenty of one
kind talked about in the media and in so-called
contemporary literature; plenty of another in the
Churches, but although the same word was used, there
seemed to be no connection between the two. Was it even
possible for her and her contemporaries to "love" the earth
or anything earthy, as distinct from desiring to consume it?
Had love itself been 'polluted'? Promptly then her
historian's instinct joined in the mêlée. *Amour Courtois* —
was that what it had all been *about*? The change of
direction, the fading of divinity from the phenomenal
world including the bodies of men and women — the call

Does "love" have multiple meanings?

on human will and human feeling to restore it from within. The end of the Iron Age and the beginning of its erosive sequelae. Had they without knowing it — the Provençal singers and lovers, the troubadours, Dante and his circle — been pioneering that restoration?

Such speculations were of course absorbing rather than painful. Indeed, they were in some ways a relief from her paramount obsession: the need for action and the obligation to take it. It was this last that was growing more and more engrossing, and its effects on her behaviour more and more noticeable, this that was threatening to ruin a marriage. She herself became increasingly aware of that threat, as she watched the effect on Leo of the change going on in herself. Both were growing more silent when they were alone together. Both, it was becoming evident, were more at ease when they were alone.

It was not that there was discord; only that detachment had turned into alienation. It was a state of affairs that Vi found harder to bear than Leo did. She knew that he was unhappy, perhaps not less so than herself. But it was she, with her greater awareness, who reached the conclusion that they were now mainly in each other's way, that their life together, as she put it herself, was *all wrong*. She pondered whether to suggest a divorce. Perhaps that *was* the solution. But first she must have one more try to make things right between them. She sought and found a favourable opportunity to share memories with him — that long day on the Down, their meeting Harry Coppard and the impression he had made on them both, then and on subsequent visits. She had felt so happy that they both felt the same about things. This time she was trying to change *his* feeling, rather than insist on her own.

But the attempt failed; there was no real response from him; and she was inwardly engaged in mustering up courage to utter the word "divorce" (inevitably it would be like firing the first shot in a battle), when something occurred that looked as if it might offer hopes of a way out.

Leonard had been making some headway in the academic world. Not only were his lectures exceptionally well attended, but he had also published two articles — mainly technical in their subject-matter but well and vigorously expressed — in learned periodicals. In the world of archaeology, even beyond the confines of the British Isles, his name was not entirely unknown. By what was no more than a coincidence, he now received by post two invitations on two successive days. The first was to participate in a two-week-long international Symposium in Florence during the approaching summer vacation. The second and more impressive one was the offer of a senior appointment in his old University of Cartishall.

Unhesitatingly they agreed that he should accept them both. They felt with relief that the activity and excitement in the immediate future and the substantial change that would follow in their outward circumstances might do something to dispel the storm cloud that was settling on their marriage. Leonard went further than that. He pondered anxiously whether he could use the opportunity to provide his wife with help of some kind, for he had been feeling that she needed help. But of *what* kind? That was the difficulty. Knowing so little of what was amiss, he knew so little of what was needed. What did she like? What did she *enjoy*? What would be best for her? Finally he wrote to a friend, who, being blessed with some private income in addition to his salary, had acquired an apartment residence in the Appenines which, when he and his wife were not occupying it, they sometimes let and sometimes offered free to their friends. Having received a satisfactory reply, he told Vi of his plan.

"I thought we might have a week's holiday there before I have to go to Florence," he said. "We could hire a car and get about a bit. Then you could either come on to Florence with me, or come back home, whichever you like." He decided not to mention at this stage a third possibility he had in mind.

Vi jumped eagerly at the suggestion. Italy! Wind's *Pagan Mysteries in the Renaissance*, Seznec's *The Survival of the Pagan Gods* — those exciting books Herapath had lent her a month or two ago! Italy! Florence and its picture galleries — Verona — Siena — Romantic Tuscany (*where* was it Dante had lived in exile?) — Ravenna — all just names to her, for she had never been to Italy. It was extraordinary how she forgot all her troubles in the excitement of anticipation and the activity of preparing for the trip. Not nearly as much time as she could have wished for reading it all up in guide-books and elsewhere.

When it came, it was even better than she had expected. They flew to Pisa and hired a car. Next, following the instructions in Leo's letter from his friend, they phoned up Giovanni in his grocer's shop in the village, to let him know

what time they were arriving; and then they were off. The
village, when they reached it, was a dream; nestling in a
valley in the upper reaches of the Arno, with its 'Borgo'
perched on top of a steep hill above it. The Borgo, once
a fortified castle, had come down in the world so far as first
to become a monastery and then to be divided up into
apartments for letting — mostly on long leases to Italians
from Florence who only came for weekends. It was one
of these apartments to which a smiling Giovanni handed
them the key, after first informing them as a fact that the
divine Dante had lived there for a time while it was still a
monastery. Later they learned that this was no more than
an unconfirmed rumour, but that did not prevent the
villagers and nearby peasant farmers from referring to the
poet as if he were still one of their neighbours. With these
honest and friendly country people (Vi had acquired
enough Italian to enable communication) they made some
acquaintance during two happy days spent wandering
through the pine-clad slopes and cypress walks out into the
surrounding country, and then Vi suggested they should
drive to at least one city. Florence could be left until they
were on their way home, but there were other towns not
too far off — Siena, for instance — where there was so
much to be seen.

So now Leonard unmasked the second part of his plan.
Although he had only taken on the apartment for a week,
he knew it was not wanted for another three weeks after
that. How would she like to stay on for a fortnight while
he was in Florence and explore all she wanted to on her
own? The proposition was rendered all the more

attractive by the circumstance that an American couple, with whom he was acquainted, were staying in another apartment in the Borgo. The husband's academic career involved his spending much time in Europe, some of it in England, where he had met Leo, and he too had acquired a *pied-à-terre* in the Borgo for occasional use. Friendly relations had already been established between the two couples. The suggestion was put forward by Leonard because he had perceptively guessed, when making his plans, that Vi's responses to works of art and historical associations would be more spontaneous if he were not there to intrude on them. He did not of course mention this; he only said, quite truthfully, that he would prefer to spend the rest of his week in the peace and quiet of their immediate surroundings.

To this, Vi, with the new perspective now opened to her, did not object. It had been a happy time for both of them, happier than they had known for a long period, and she was glad enough to have it continue. Indeed the day fixed for his departure came sooner than she could have wished. But it did come, and she was now alone and 'free' in a way she had never known before. She made good use of her fortnight. Petrol was cheap and she liked driving. Siena, Padua, Assisi, Montepulciano — she found her way to all of them. But what she liked even better than these visits, with the hours of driving they involved, was to take the car out and potter at random through the country nearer at hand, never knowing what she might find — a mountain village, a half-hidden church, even an un-Baedekered little town. It was in this way that she came quite by accident

on the Franciscan monastery perched on its hill at La
Verna. But the most memorable of all her discoveries was
hidden away in a church in a little town, not far from
Arezzo, whose name she did not even know, not a
particularly attractive town either.

CHAPTER VI

VI HAD HARDLY realised as yet how fertile and withal how prodigal the Italian artists of the Renaissance had been. So much so that you may still find, tucked away in some inconspicuous corner, a little known masterpiece by one of the Master's pupils, or even by the Master himself. The church was for the most part ill-lit, but high on one wall, with a facing window to throw light on it, was a fresco, at which she stood staring, or rather gazing, for a long time. It was of the Resurrection. She noted every detail, almost as if — although she had no such intention — she were trying to memorise it. For the rock-closed cave indicated by the Gospel record, the painter had substituted a rectangular marble tomb. In front of it, at ground level, sprawled four sleeping soldiers. Sleeping? The painter had somehow managed to convey the impression of a deplorable apathy. Or was one of them deliberately hiding his eyes with both hands? Behind them, with one raised foot resting on the tomb, startlingly erect and half as tall as the whole picture, stood the figure of the Christ. Risen. Not only the sternly upright posture was emphasising that, but perhaps even more its colour, sharply contrasted with the dull blues, greens and browns of the soldiers' garments. What colour? Not any ordinary flesh-tint for the half-wrapped body, nor any ordinary 'pink' for the robe that hung from one shoulder — rather two neighbouring shades merging gently into one another, and both of the same ineffable brightness. And then, behind it the sketched suggestion of a living natural world, its trees and shrubs, its low hills and lightly clouded sky.

At last she had looked her fill and took her leave, aware only that no picture, no work of art or literature, had ever thrilled her so. And yet 'thrilled' was too weak a word; say rather excited — moved, as she only came to realise later, to the depths of her being. Only as she was driving home did she recall one little touch that few would probably notice, and to which she herself had paid no conscious attention at the time. The face of the tomb was decorated near its foot with the marble head of a lion. It reminded her now — had it subconsciously reminded her as soon as she noticed it? — of the lion's head they had seen years ago at the mouth of Eager Spring.

Two days later she was back again. This time it was late in the afternoon, and the light within the Church was warmer. Otherwise all was as before, except that the colours of the robe and the flesh of the risen Christ seemed to her even more mysterious. This time, too, her attention became riveted on the countenance. It gazed straight down at her. Later on she was to reflect that, if she had been asked to describe its expression, she must have been hard put to it to find words. How was it possible for the artist to have conveyed, through the dark eyes and the calm mouth, that impression of a being who had come through — everything... ? Vi had never thought much about the actual meaning of those words "and he overcame death"; but the image before her seemed to be compelling her to ask, What do they mean? Again it was only when reflecting on it later that she hit on such phrases as "not in the least authoritarian" ... "it leaves me free" ... "it seems to ask, What am I to you?" For the present she simply looked and felt. At last she lowered her gaze to the lion's head. Eager Spring, yes, but it was also similar to other lion's heads that gushed forth water in many a village piazza — and, with that, inner and outer rushed together in her mind. Water was life, the life of plants and birds and beasts. But here was a greater Life, a Life the soldiers hunched their shoulders against, or hid their eyes from, a Life that gazed from the lifeless wall seeming to say: "What am I to you?"

She sat on for a long time as the light faded, looking now not at the fresco but at her own hands resting in her lap, hands fashioned to do, touch, write at the dictate of her will. Then she raised her eyes again to that unfathomable gaze. Was a mere work of art shaming her into a sense of her own passivity and all-round imperfection? Anyway it was time to leave now. Yet she lingered a few minutes longer speculating. Was it the artist speaking through his subject — or the subject speaking through the artist? Did the command, 'You must live differently,' come to her from within the picture, or did it pass into the picture from within her own stirred spirit?

And then, during the drive home, there came another question. Living differently must mean, among other things, living differently with Leo, living differently as a wife. Ought she not to begin that by at least trying to share with him what she had just been going through? She envisaged the kind of conversation it would mean, her attempts to explain and his painfully unsuccessful effort to

Life: what am I to you?

go along with her. In the end — and still unhappily
doubtful whether it was wisdom or cowardice that turned
the scale — she decided to say nothing about it, on the
ground of a certain sacred, or even sacramental quality in
it, which could only be diminished — or was 'betrayed' the
word? — by any attempt to communicate it to anyone,
even to a husband or lover.

Right or wrong, wise or unwise, the decision was
probably biased by an impressive dream she had had. She
had indeed had more than one qualitatively unusual dream
during those two weeks of unwonted grass-widowhood.
There was, for instance, the one that seemed to be
concerned with nothing but colours: simply that she was
breathing in red air and breathing out blue. In a second
one she was looking at a delightful prospect in front of her.
In a soft, bright light a number of serenely dignified figures
stood with their faces towards her, and yet seemed to be
conversing with one another. She knew that they were
beyond all sorrow. All that was necessary was to step
forward and join them — except that between herself and
them, as she now for the first time noticed, there was a
black, bottomless chasm with no bridge across it; and she
awoke knowing that she was quite cut off from them.

But a third dream was the most memorable. She was
descending some rough and irregular steps that led down
into the earth. Apparently there would be something
important at the bottom of them. The steps kept growing
rougher and steeper. Nevertheless, for all her growing
anxiety, she decided to keep on. Then she heard a sound
in front of her. Someone who had descended further was

coming up again. It was Leo. "Is it dangerous?" she asked him. "Yes, of course it is," he said in a matter-of-fact voice, and continued on his way up; and she knew he meant that he had turned back before reaching the bottom. With that, the whole furniture of the dream had changed in the abrupt yet smooth way that is characteristic of dreams. She was alone in empty space, in terror of falling into unfathomed depths below. Suddenly she realised the presence, within her reach, of a strong, straight metal rod let down from above. She clung to it with all her might, and the terror vanished. She heard, above and around her, not so much a voice as a ringing made of words, words with a rising intonation, words that began loud as a shout and gradually reverberated away into a silence that was alive:

"DIVINE IRE ᴵ HOLD … divine ire … divine ire …"

She awoke with precisely those words still ringing in her ears; clear, distinct, unforgettable — but what did they mean? Distinct — and yet *ire* was a strange word to come in there. Was she quite sure it had not been *iron*?

The two days that followed her second visit to the Church were something of an anti-climax, and she was quite glad the time had now come for their return to England. Leo had arranged accommodation for her for one night in Florence, so that they could leave early on the following morning. She left the village soon after dawn, and reached Florence by mid-day — in time for a long afternoon in the Uffizi, where she kept that appointment with the Botticellis which she had purposely been saving to the last.

So ended the Italian interlude, for that was what it looked like to her in retrospect. The return journey was uneventful, but Leo was in good spirits and had much to tell her about his experiences at the Conference. What had impressed him most, it seemed, were the slides shown by one of the lecturers, who had been concerned in excavations recently conducted in another part of Tuscany. The expedition had unearthed what were perhaps the earliest examples of Etruscan sculpture — if sculpture was the right word for the at first sight shapeless blocks they had turned up. One theory was that one of them at least was a meteorite, that it had been lightly worked to suggest human features, and that the others were attempts to imitate it.

CHAPTER VII

FOR THE NEXT few weeks both of them were kept busy and — what made easier Vi's problem of 'living differently' at home — both were pleasantly excited. For Vi there was all the business of partial redecoration, of arranging their furniture to the best effect, which would involve throwing two rooms into one, and of the anxious consideration and discussions with Leo that all this involved. For Leo there was a novel routine to get used to, new colleagues to meet and assimilate and a good deal of reading to make up on, since part of his new syllabus covered an area he had not taught before. And that also meant preparing new lectures. Almost it seemed they were back in the first year of their marriage.

When, after a few weeks, they found themselves more at leisure, they decided, and Vi was never sure which of them first suggested it, to spend a day on the downs; and to cover the same ground as they had done on that walk long ago, when they had made the acquaintance of Harry Coppard. It would be good to find out if he was still alive and well in his cottage. So as before, they turned off the road and started up the slope by the path that ran near Eager Spring; and as before they made the little detour. But this time, as soon as the spring came in sight, Vi let out a little yelp of surprise. The brushwood round it had all been cleared away, leaving it conspicuous at the head of a little oblong plot of grass. Someone had even scraped the blotches of moss from the lion's head. But that was not all. It was not even the most delightful part of the surprise. The spring was flowing again! A small but steady stream of clear water was falling from the lion's mouth into an equally clear rivulet that meandered across the grass plot and disappeared into the bushes. Underneath the lion a metal cup was fastened by a chain. "Just look!" said Vi, and she was pointing now, not to the mouth of the spring but at the rivulet. Someone, the moss-eradicator perhaps, or perhaps the children from that cottage on the road, had planted wild flowers along both sides of it.

"Wonderful!" said Leo as they both stood gazing. "After all those years! I wonder how it happened." But when they reached the higher ground and were approaching nearer to Harry's cottage, he thought perhaps the mystery was explaining itself. The 'spewy heath', as the contemptuous Cobbett once called it in his *Rural Rides*, was spewy no longer. More and more, as they went forward, they found themselves walking through a little wood, or rather a little nursery of young oak trees, which would one day be a wood, even perhaps a forest. Until at last they reached the older plantation of birch and hawthorn and the like, with there at the end of the glade, Harry's cottage just as they remembered it. And covering the rising ground behind it, more and more baby forest as far as the eye could reach.

Harry had seen them coming and opened the door to greet them. He looked older, but there was nothing decrepit about him, and they were soon engaged in eager conversation. First about the trees. Yes, he had gone on with his sowing for a few years after he last saw them, but had at last to give it up. He felt he had done his stint. What did they think of them? Vi was almost lyrical in her enthusiasm. Leo nodded an emphatic assent, and went on to tell of their surprise at the change in Eager Spring. Harry, who did not walk so far nowadays, was pleased. He had heard a year or two before some rumours of water reappearing, but not that it had become a regular flow. He had no doubt that the effect of his trees on the soil was responsible for it. He could really feel, then, that he had done something, however small, to "stop the rot", as he called it. Inevitably the conversation led to a more general canvassing of what he called the rot, and Vi called the rape of the earth. She was soon asking him if he knew anything of the Earth-lovers and telling him of her experience with them in the Midlands. Yes, they were quite strong in this part of the world, he said, and appeared to be increasing. He had met some of them not long since, when they asked permission to camp for a night or two on his ground. On the whole his impression was favourable. He had not had much to do with them, but he was glad there were such people about. It was clear from the way he spoke that he had some reservations, but he did not voice them. It was only later that Vi came to realise their nature.

They were both rather silent on the way home. Leo had hoped his wife had forgotten about the Earth-lovers and all that went with them; he had been sorry to hear her raise the subject, was wondering if she had simply been making conversation, or if it meant more than that, and was speculating vaguely on the future. He might well do so, for Vi's mind was full of it. Suddenly the Italian interlude seemed a long way off, and the continuity with her life before it was restored. The following day she took herself to task; 'living differently' surely ought not to mean giving up all that side, her responsibility as a human being for the present and the future. Surely it was the other way round. The difference should begin to show itself by enhancing the feeble effect that was all she had so far given to the impulse towards something more actual. Gradually, as the days passed, her perspective shifted. The academic part of her looked less important. As for that book she had had at the back of her mind, she let it go. Perhaps, some day, when she was much older, she might write something — but not necessarily as a contribution to scholarship. There were other things to be done than cultivating her own spirit. And so, admittedly without much enthusiasm and with some sighs of renunciation, she embarked on the first other thing she could think of. She called on the secretary to the Earth-lovers.

It was clear from the very first meeting she attended that they were very different from the group in the Midlands. More determined and more vigorous. But for that reason more frustrated. 'Protest' was the word most in use among them, whether it was protest against local development infringing the Green Belt or delegated participation in protests nationally organised against industrial and political threats on a large scale. They were of no particular social class, and in theory at any rate, of no one political persuasion. But Vi soon discovered that the most energetic and active members were radical, if not revolutionary, in their opinions. Some of the political demonstrations which they persuaded the group to join, and in which they would offer to represent the group by participating personally, had little to do with loving the

earth, much with the compulsory reform of society,
whether at home or abroad, on egalitarian lines. There
were one or two strident feminists among them. And she
was shrewd enough to perceive that there were others who
really did not care much what was to be protested against
as long as it was authorised by a government in office
somewhere, or what kind of demonstration the group
supported as long as it was likely to entail physical violence.
Never mind. The group as a whole was genuinely
concerned to do something pointing away from sickness
and towards health; and who was she to draw her
fastidious skirts about her and pass by?

Now she thought she divined the nature of Harry
Coppard's unspoken reservations; and it led her to reflect
that there was something else she could do that she felt sure
would be right. She could keep in touch with him. If the
atmosphere at group meetings was sometimes rather
stifling, his company was like fresh air, and she made a
point of visiting him as often as she could. It did not
matter much what they talked of or if, as they sometimes
did, they simply sat in silence. Yet he had plenty to say,
and it was during this period that Vi learned a good deal
about the early history of the iron industry and the
significance of 'hammer ponds' and other vestiges of it
that lingered in the nomenclature and the contours of the
district. It was always refreshing to be with him. During
one of her visits he accidentally threw light on an allusion
that had sometimes puzzled her in her dealings with the
group. The words "the dump" were apt to occur in their
utterances and Vi, who was somewhat shy, had never

plucked up courage to ask what exactly they meant, since it was taken for granted that everyone, who *was* anyone, knew that already. "You might as well say the dump doesn't matter," someone would say; and Vi would have a guilty feeling that the speaker was referring to some esoteric principle in the aims of the group about which it would be naive to enquire.

They had been talking of the general state of agriculture, or 'agri-business', as it had become, throughout the world. Harry Coppard compared it to one vast farm, or rather one huge machine, put into gear and then 'controlled', as it was supposed, by what used to be called a 'governor' in the early days of machinery — those two revolving balls that slowed the engine when it speeded up too much. First hasten and intensify growth with ethylene, and then slow it down again with biocides. That was all there was to it.

Since he had become more confined to the house, Harry had rather reluctantly acquired a radio, and was in many respects more in touch with what was going on in the world than his visitor. By the kindness of a distant neighbour he was also kept supplied, if at rather irregular intervals, with a quality newspaper. It was when he had gone on to a more topical issue that he had let drop the puzzling word. A new and particularly effective biocide had recently been discovered, and then quickly manufactured on a large scale. Particularly effective, but also particularly dangerous. He hunted up a copy he had obtained of a leaflet that accompanied the containers in which it was supplied, and read her a few extracts from it:

"Wear rubber gloves and face shield ... remove heavily contaminated clothing immediately ... wash hands and exposed skin before eating, drinking or smoking after work ... harmful to livestock. Keep all livestock out of treated areas for at least two weeks ... harmful to game, wild birds and animals ... harmful to bees ... harmful to fish" etc. etc. And then, under separate headings: "Symptoms of Poisoning. First Aid Treatment. Guide for the Doctor."

There had been news, not very widely disseminated, of small farmers whose cows had suddenly begun dying off for no perceptible reason, or had started producing only half their normal milk. None of the farmers had actually used the new preparation. But it was argued that it was being used by larger farms not far off. As soon as a link between the new preparation and the sporadic disasters had been suggested, the 'Green' people and associated pressure groups had vociferously demanded its suppression. Supported by its manufacturers and their adroit lobbying enthusiasts, who identified all technological advance with progressive evolution, had contended that no such link had been established, there was not sufficient evidence, and so forth. But pressure had continued to increase none the less and, when a private member's Bill was introduced in parliament to make the use of the preparation illegal, although it would probably not have survived its second reading, feeling both in the House and in the country was so strong that the Government had decided to compromise. They had offered an amendment which would temporarily outlaw it, pending a full-scale Inquiry. Meanwhile all existing stocks would be 'dumped' in certain relatively remote spots with special precautions to prevent any of it escaping by seepage or otherwise. The Bill so amended had been passed and the dumping had duly taken place, but nothing had been heard of the Inquiry. Harry indeed suspected that nothing more *would* be heard of it, or not for a long time. The government was dragging its feet in the hope that the problem would go away.

Meanwhile the location of the dumps was being kept as secret as possible, and it was only by accident that on one of his walks he had come, in an unfrequented part of the heath, on a curious formation; a high circular bank, which might have been taken for the remains of a British Camp, if it were not for the fact that the bank on its outer side was surrounded by close netting topped with barbed wire. He had no doubt that it was one of them. No, he was not specially concerned about its proximity to his own dwelling. For one thing he had no livestock except his bees, and he did not depend on them for a livelihood. It was not so much this particular dump that worried him, but the dumps in general, both in themselves and as a symptom of what was going on all round. Harry was not a chemist, at any rate not an up-to-date one; and he was no expert in the string of impossibly long names, generally ending in -amine, or -ylene, or -ide, with the help of which it was conducted. But there was one thing on which he was very emphatic. For all the plethora of long names, modern chemistry did not, he said, really *know* anything. They might conduct controlling experiments or make tests that showed a preparation to be reassuringly harmless. But the harmlessness thus established only extends to immediately consequential effects. Of the long-term effects they could well be having, not only on plants and livestock but also on the human beings who consumed them, they knew nothing and could know nothing until another twenty or thirty years had elapsed. His mind was not so much on the local dump as on the rapidly increasing proliferation of herbicides in particular and agrochemicals in general. Above all, what was being dangerously overlooked was the unknown consequence of one chemical agent uniting with matter already impregnated by another. He stepped to his bookshelf and took down Rachel Carson's *The Silent Spring*. "Listen," he said:

> Perhaps most important of all for the future, though very little indeed is known about them at present, are the possible interactions between freely mixed chemicals, such as are now getting into the soil, into the rivers and lakes, and indeed into the oceans, an interaction which is building up the whole time. ... these reactions may be between two or more chemicals, or between chemicals and the radio-active wastes that are being discharged in ever increasing volume. Under the impact of ionizing radiation some rearrangement of atoms could easily occur, changing the nature of the chemicals in a way that is not only unpredictable, but beyond control.

"They think they know everything, and they really know nothing," he added, as he closed the book and returned it to the shelf. "In that farm affair — where was it? Smarden? — they turned guinea-pig cows loose on the suspected herbage, and they all died of poisoning, although no trace of fluorocetamide was detectable in it."

Vi had much to turn over in her mind as she made her way home; and, later on, much to say to her fellow Earth-lovers, who at that time were interesting themselves especially in a number of cases of inexplicable sickness that had been occurring in the local population. They were vaguely suspicious — and vague suspicion was a substantial ingredient in their stock-in trade — that toxicity from pollution had something to do with it. But they had no evidence. It was this circumstance that induced Vi to decide to pay another visit to Coppard and discuss it with him. This time she would take another member of the group with her, the woman with whom she felt most affinity and with whom she had struck up something like a friendship.

A week or two later, as they set out together, Vi casually asked her friend, whose name was Jennifer, if she had ever discovered Eager Spring. No. She had not. "Let's have a look at it on the way up, then," said Vi, and they turned aside accordingly. But any secret notion she may have been nursing that there was a treat in store for Jennifer, was soon to be knocked on the head. The flowers on the grass plot, when they reached it, were all withered, and the chained cup had been removed. But that was not all. Around the lion's head, from which the spring emerged, a cage of netting had been fixed, and above it a pegged notice-board on which was inscribed the warning: NO WATER TO BE CONSUMED UNTIL FURTHER NOTICE. For a few moments they looked at each other without a word; and then they resumed their uphill journey.

CHAPTER VIII

COPPARD, WHEN JENNIFER had been introduced and they had told him what had been found, only nodded his head. He was evidently much more interested in the news *he* had to impart to them. Since Vi's last visit, and perhaps partly because of it, he had begun to interest himself a little in the dump and what was going on there. Apparently the procedure was for lorries to arrive by a rough track from the nearest road and to deliver their load, which consisted of good-sized wooden crates. These were taken inside and what happened after that he was of course unable to see. He had however managed to get into conversation with one of the lorry-drivers who told him that, as he understood it, the crates were packed with the material officially ordered to be dumped; this was emptied from the crates, and, he supposed, either stacked or buried in some way. On its return journey each lorry carried a load of empty crates, which could no doubt be used again. Harry paused at this point as though something had just occurred to him. "Empty," he said. "I wonder!"

He went on to tell them something else. Some weeks back, before he knew anything about the dump, at some distance from his house, beside a road, he had noticed a wooden packing-case. At that point the road was raised on a kind of low causeway, that had been banked across a patch of marshy ground. He had assumed the case contained furniture, or something of the sort, and that it had somehow fallen off the vehicle that carried it, perhaps because that had swerved over the side of the causeway.

Probably it had had to pass a car coming the other way. He also noticed the case had been smashed open in one place, where it had fallen or rolled onto a large stone. The fact that on one side of it, presumably the top when it was right side up, was nailed a consignment label with an address in Central Africa, seemed to confirm his surmise that it had to do with the transport of someone's private effects. When he returned next day, the case had been taken away. Later, he had had that conversation with the lorry-driver near the dump; the man had told him that, yes, it was one of their empty crates on its way back to the manufacturers, that had fallen off its lorry. "So no harm done!" the man had added, with a smile on his face that Coppard did not altogether like.

Since then he had thought about it all a good deal and wondered if the man had been telling the truth. The fact that the crate had fallen off the road on its left hand side did seem to confirm his story that the blundering lorry was on its way out and not in, and therefore the crate *was* presumably empty. But then, how to explain the consignment label? An old one that had been left on from some previous use? But it didn't *look* old; nor did the crate. He had shrugged off the conundrum.

But now he stopped and looked hard at his two visitors.

"That long marshy patch," he said, "never quite dries up now. I don't know why. There must be some kind of water table underneath that keeps it damp — perhaps a small spring or two pokes up into it. It did use to dry up from time to time before my trees got going, but not now. And now I'll tell you another thing," he said after a pause.

"I'm fairly sure that patch is in the catchment area that feeds your Eager Spring. I don't do it now but, when I was younger, I used to walk all over the heath and its surroundings, trying to get to know what you people call its ecology. I had to. It was the only way I could decide on the best places for my acorns."

For a time they all sat silent. "What can be done?" asked Vi at last, and Harry closed his eyes for a moment, thinking. Then:

"The first thing," he said, "must be to find out more. And it won't be easy. There may be a lot of well-placed people interested in our *not* finding out more."

Easy or not, by the time they left him an hour later, the three had sketched, at least in outline, a plan of action.

On their way home the women decided they must begin by taking the obvious step. So the following afternoon they called at the offices of the Local Authority and, after being referred from one Department to another and from that to a third, they were shown into a room containing a young man behind a desk, who politely asked them their business. They would like to know, they said, whether the Authority was responsible for the Notice closing Eager Spring to the public. Yes, it was. Could he tell them why?

"Wait a minute," he said, and took a notebook out of a drawer in his desk. "Yours is the first enquiry we've had on that," he said apologetically as he turned the pages of the notebook, and then, looking up from it:

"We found the water was slightly polluted in some way. We think it's diesel spillage from a farm above it. We've asked them to see if there's a leak in their storage tank.

Once the spillage is stopped the trouble will gradually right itself."

Vi was on the point of asking him whether their Health Department suspected any connection between the pollution and the recent outbreak of unexplained sickness among children in the neighbourhood, which had been the subject of correspondence and comment in the local press. But she restrained herself and remained silent.

"Did you believe him?" Jennifer asked, as soon as they got outside.

"He may have hoped it was true," said Vi, "but I'm pretty sure it wasn't."

Anyhow the way was now clear for the main plan to go ahead.

In advising them on this, old Coppard had shown that he had not forgotten all the management skills he had had to acquire during those early years in his father's business. He knew how to clarify future requirements by classifying them. "There are two problems," he had said. "First we must find out exactly what is happening; and secondly, if we find it is bad or dangerous, we must get cast-iron evidence of it. Any attempt to bring things into the open, based on mere suspicion, would only play into their hands. I'll give you all the help I can."

And then he told them something else he had just remembered. The lorry-driver he had questioned had not only said, "So no harm done." He had added: "Anyway it's not for them to make a song and dance about careful handling. If you'd seen the smashed crates *inside* the compound — two of them — with the guts spilling out!"

government cover up

As to the crate he had found beside the road, the single push he now remembered giving it proved it was much too heavy to be empty. So there were full crates as well as empty ones *leaving* the dump. Why?

He had gone on to point out that the first requirement could itself be subdivided. First, to prove whether the stored biocide or other substance was in fact having a disseminated toxic effect on the soil around it at a lower level, and secondly to find out why some of it was being carted out again, and where it went to. "And it looks," he said, "as if the best way of solving problem number one is to get a first-class professional analysis of a sample of the water coming out of Eager Spring."

It was this first step that Vi now set out to achieve. She began by taking Leo into her confidence. He was decidedly uneasy about the whole project, but he was anxious to maintain the better relations that had followed the Italian interlude and, although in no way committed like his wife, he could not feel entirely indifferent to its social implications or to the responsibility which knowledge, or even surmise, of mortal danger involves. So he approached a colleague in the Department of Science. Perhaps he did so in rather a shamefaced way, indicating a need to humour a wife who rather badly needed humouring just now. Anyway he did it. And the upshot was that Vi and Jennifer, with the help of a pair of wire-cutters and without much difficulty, obtained a small bottle filled from Eager Spring, which found its way to a well-placed friend of Leo's colleague in a prestigious chemical research institute. The result was not long in coming. In his accompanying letter the eminent chemist had written:

"There is nothing in the trace elements, nothing unusual that is, except that they do apparently include a minute trace of X." And he had added in a postscript on a separate sheet: "X = the unknown. All I do know is, that it is one of the components in that proprietary 'agri-product' which was the subject of the Bill recently before parliament. You will not be surprised that I don't know what it is, since, as you will have read or heard more than once on TV or radio, no-one else does either. Nor, thanks to the secrets clause in the Trades Description legislation, do we even know how it is obtained."

Vi and Jennifer lost no time in reporting this initial result to Coppard, and it was agreed that the next step must now follow. It was very much more formidable than the first. This time the plan of campaign required the help of the group as a whole, or at all events of its active members. There was an argumentative, if not a stormy, meeting, but eventually a sufficient number volunteered, and among them Vi herself. Partly because the initiative had come from her, but partly also because she was good-looking, she was appointed to the place of danger. She was to be, in the fullest sense of the word, the protagonist.

It would be unkind to expatiate on the qualms she suffered after accepting the post of honour. For one thing it involved acting a part, and she was no actress by either experience or inclination. But there was more to it than that. It is all very well for Cyrano de Bergerac to proclaim "Mais on n'abdique pas l'honneur d'être une cible," but we are not all Cyranos. It was no use trying to summon up *panache* from the depths of her being, for she had none. And in any case *panache* is an essentially masculine gift. What did keep her from backing out at the last minute — before it was too late — was the memory of that picture in the church in Tuscany — and of her last dream.

With the first move of all she was not directly involved. A few members of the group who possessed cars were detailed to follow some of the lorries leaving the dump, of course at a discreet distance, and to report their destination. They did so, and there was no mystery about it. Three out of four of them, approximately, turned into the London Road. To remove all doubts one of these was followed for another thirty miles or so, and there was little doubt that they were taking empty crates back to the manufacturers. But the fourth, it was discovered, went to Southampton, where the crates disappeared into the yard of a shipping company. What happened to them after that was beyond the reach of the sleuths. But in two instances, by exercising no little ingenuity, they did manage to see and make a note of the consignment labels. One of these was to an address in Uganda, the other to Honduras. They knew now therefore that, in addition to the lorries used for conveying empties back to London, there were some that carried loaded crates for export, for export in the only two cases they had checked, to the third world.

And now it was nearly time for Vi's own ordeal. Not quite. First came the rehearsals, of which there must be a good many, since any blunder might well be disastrous. Altogether a considerable time elapsed while all this was going forward, and Spring was now well advanced. There was plenty of time for the qualms to repeat themselves. Once during the waiting period, Vi had had another dream that approached in significance the ones she had had in Tuscany. In it she saw a tawny African lion pacing across the hills. It sank slowly into squashy, polluted soil, tried to draw out its paws and roared in agony. The roar awoke her, and she fell asleep and dreamed again, this time that she was part of a landscape that seemed somehow familiar to her, though she could not say why. She knew that, if she walked up a path between some trees, she would come to a place called "the Dance Ground". But there was barbed wire across the path, and she could not get to it. She had a strong feeling that there was something behind her. Turning, she saw another lion who was both old and young, he was white like stone but at the same time slightly luminous, like alabaster, and she knew that he was the guardian of Eager Spring, and was glad that he was behind her.

But now at last the time for qualms and dreams was over and the time for action had come.

CHAPTER IX

THE LORRY WAS bowling along a major road that led to a motorway. Evening was drawing in. It was overtaking a girl with tousled hair, striding along in her open-neck T-shirt and bravely patched jeans, with a rucksack on her back. She turned before it reached her and held up her thumb with an ingratiating smile. The driver stopped and asked her where she was making for, and she mentioned a village some five miles farther on. He nodded, and she climbed on board and at once asked him where *he* was bound for. "London," he said.

"Do you do the journey every day?"

"No," he said, "I shan't be on this tomorrow."

The rest of their conversation is immaterial, but if the driver had been a little sharper, he would have noticed a slight incident that occurred a mile or two further on. About the middle of a long straight stretch of road, they passed a minor turning off to the left. Some way beyond, but well within sight of it, they passed a stationary estate car, facing them on their right, with four young people in it. What the driver did not notice was that, as they approached it, his passenger gave a very slight shake of her head.

The following evening, at about the same time, history repeated itself. The same girl was walking along the same stretch of road. Once again a lorry overtook her, and once again she begged a lift and got it. And just as before, as soon as she had climbed on board, she asked the driver where he was bound for. This time the reply was Southampton, and from that time on history was far from

repeating itself. You would have thought it was a different
girl altogether, a voluble and rather larky one. Almost
before he had started up again she was telling him all about
herself, how she loved hitch-hiking, how she had hitch-
hiked through half the countries in Europe. Some found
it difficult, but she never had any trouble — perhaps
because she knew how to pay a chap for helping her on.
"But I'm talking too much," she said. "Oh gosh, I always
do." She stopped — it was just before they came in sight
of the turning on the left — and looked at him with the
mischievously inviting smile she had practised so carefully
before a mirror. "Don't you sometimes want a rest?" she
suggested. "You must be tired after all that driving." And
she added, "There must be a side road somewhere." The
driver nodded vigorously and, when the signpost came in
sight, he slowed down and turned into the side road.

There was another respect in which history *had* been
repeating itself: a little way beyond the turning the same
estate car, with the same four young people in it, had been
waiting. Now it started up, two of its occupants got out,
and it began driving slowly up the same side road, keeping
well behind the lorry, which was itself progressing very
slowly, with the driver looking out for an opening in the
woodland on either side where the lorry could be left
standing for a while. Further in among the trees the two
who had descended from the estate car came hurrying in
the same direction at nearly the same pace. When at last
the lorry came to a convenient gap, the girl nudged the
driver. He nodded, drew well into the side of the road and
opened the off-side door to descend. But the girl did not

open her door, because at that moment there was the blare
of a horn and the estate car rushed past at a disgracefully
excessive speed. It rounded a bend in the road in front,
and immediately there was an ominous thumping noise
followed by loud cries of dismay. By this time the driver
had descended from the lorry and was standing on the
road beside it. "You stay here, darling," he said. "I'll just
go and see what's up."

No sooner had he disappeared round the bend than the
two passengers from the estate car emerged into the road,
out of breath with running. They jumped into the back
of the lorry, where Vi was already busy. Her job was to see
as many as were accessible of the labels on the crates and
memorise the destinations. The other two, each armed
with a jemmy, got to work on the most conveniently stacked
crate and ripped off a plank. Vi had done her job and was
eagerly watching. She peered inside and saw that it was full
of sealed plastic bags. She tried to pull one out. It was too
big for the gap. The men heaved up a second plank, and
she found she could just squeeze one of the bags out of the
crate. "Hurry! Hurry!" they were whispering to her, as if
she didn't know that time was precious! But their agitation
added to her own, and she did not notice that the bag had
caught on a nail and split slightly as she dragged it out, and
before she hurriedly stuffed it into her capacious rucksack,
while the other two restored the crate, as nearly as they
could, to its former condition.

Meanwhile the two remaining occupants of the estate
car had been struggling, with the help of the lorry-driver,
to heave it out of the roadside ditch into which it had

swerved. Apparently it was too heavy for them, and they were considering giving up, when luckily, round the bend in the road that hid the lorry from them they saw two men and a girl approaching. One of the exhausted man-handlers waved and beckoned to them.

"I say," he called out, when they were near enough, "could you give us a hand? The five of us together ought to be able to hump the beastly thing back again." And, with a good deal of panting and swearing, they did at last manage to lift the car back onto the road.

"Lucky these two stalwarts were out for their evening stroll, just then," said Vi, a little breathlessly. Was breathlessness catching? *She* had not been violently exerting herself. The driver of the car got into it, to see if any damage showed, and started the engine. He stopped it again. "Seems to be O.K.," he said through the window to the others, who were standing round recovering their breath, while one of them wiped his forehead with a handkerchief. The lorry-driver, who was looking at Vi, made a motion of his head in the direction from which they had come, just as the man in the car put his head out and said: "Where are you making for?"

"Cartishall," said one of the new arrivals.

"And you?" he asked Vi.

"Golly," she said, "that goes for me too."

"Then you'd all better jump in."

Vi looked at the lorry-driver, and then at her watch. "It *is* getting rather late," she said, "may I?"

But the man had been getting suspicious. "But they're going in the opposite direction!" he said, and they explained to him that they were merely taking a traffic-free alternative route.

"Oh," he said, "is that so?" And there followed something like a sulky wrangle, in the course of which the lorry-driver went so far as to wonder what the pack of them were up to. At last, mollified by a five-pound note in acknowledgment of his help, he turned back along the road towards his lorry, and the car went off in the opposite direction. After about a mile, at a healthy distance now from the scene of the 'accident', it stopped, and the five occupants looked at one another.

"Whew!" said the driver. And they all turned and looked at Vi. "Well?"

She pulled out her rucksack from beneath her feet and held it up with one hand beneath it. "I've got what we want," she said; and then, turning a little pale, "It's *damp*!"

They wanted to have a look at their booty there and then. But Vi said: "I'd rather wait till we get back. Meanwhile you'd all better keep away from it. And from me," she added — "as far as possible."

To break the uneasy silence that followed, one of the men said he wondered if the driver had looked into the back of his lorry, when he got back to it, and if so what he was thinking now.

"I suppose we don't quite know what trouble we are in for!" said another.

"Not to worry!" said the driver. "His employers will never dare to bring the police into it. Think of all that would come out once an inquiry was started!"

ominous

CHAPTER X

VI WAS AWARE of having stirred slightly — very slightly. She had moved one of her legs an inch or so. It was her first moment of consciousness, and at the same time she became aware of an enormous weight pressing on her. Could she stand it? Was it going to crush her out of existence? She tried an experiment, and found that she could also move the other leg. Reassurance. Perhaps the weight was only this terrific weariness. She did not trouble to open her eyes and almost immediately was asleep again.

A few doors down the corridor, in another room in the hospital an overworked doctor was talking with Leo:

"I think," he was saying, "in fact I am pretty sure your wife passed the crisis in the early hours of this morning. She should recover consciousness at any time now."

He was wondering how to bring the conference to an end. "Go in and have a look at her."

Leo went along the passage and very softly opened the door of her room. He went in and stood looking down at her. She was lying on her back with her eyes shut, breathing peacefully. He was about to turn and tiptoe out of the room, when the eyes opened. She seemed to be looking at him in a bewildered sort of way, and he wondered if he should say something. What? "Can you speak to me?" or something like that perhaps. But before he could make up his mind the bewildered look vanished, and she smiled at him.

Leo never forgot that smile. A poet — and Leo was no poet — might perhaps have written something about the light that suddenly brims a whole landscape, when the sun breaks unexpectedly through a gap in evening clouds. If he had also had an analytical mind — and some poets do have one — he might have tried to be more explicit, babbling of how it seemed in some obscure way to be asking his forgiveness for any pains or distresses she had ever caused him, and yet at the same time to be forgiving *him* — dismissing them as if they were some kind of joke — for any she might have suffered. If he had been no poet but simply a scholar in the Humanities Department, ever on the look out for an aptly illustrative quotation, maybe he would have recalled a couple of lines from one of Dante's sonnets:

> Quel ch'ella par quand' un poco sorride
> Non si può dicer nè tener a mente.[1]

He suppressed an impulse to stoop and kiss her. Somehow it was not that kind of smile. "Can you – " he began, but she had already closed her eyes and was asleep again.

He went back to the doctor and told him that he had found her conscious at last but not disposed to talk, and that he had made no attempt to rouse her.

"Quite right," said the doctor. "She mustn't be hurried back to life. Frankly, Mr. Brook, we didn't expect her to get back. We thought the amount of the toxic agent, whatever it is, that she must have absorbed indicated an irreversible process."

---

[1] But what she seems when she a little smiles
Cannot be told or held fast in the mind.

Leo took a deep breath. "She'll pull through then?" He cleared his throat, for the question had come out as a kind of croak.

"Frankly," began the doctor — it seemed to be a favourite word. *Was* he being frank? Some doctors had that idea of 'protecting' not only the patient but the relatives as well, from the shock of truth. "Frankly, our experience of the effects of this practically unknown agent is still limited. Animal tests exhibit an unexplained variety of resistance. But there are certain widely applicable remedies that are always worth trying. Sometimes they work and sometimes they don't. In your wife's case, I am glad to say, it looks as if they are working."

Leo was relieved. The man evidently did mean what he had said. Freed of strain, his mind reverted for a moment to the whole sorry story.

"These 'generally applicable remedies'," he said, "how widely are they known?"

"Hardly at all. Some clinics in the United States and in a few European countries. You were lucky."

"So that, if some farm-worker or peasant in the third world absorbed a few drops of the stuff ... oh well, never mind!"

The doctor smiled grimly and turned down his thumb. "Perhaps they'll come up with something better before there's time to think about that. And now, if you don't mind – " he looked at his watch.

It was a long long trail. The morning after her adventure with the lorry and its driver Vi had collapsed. Giddy and sick, with violent pains in her stomach, her vision blurred and her mind growing momently more confused, she had been rushed to hospital and at once put under sedation. For two days she had continued unconscious, but it was now that she was conscious again and in no immediate danger, that the long trail began. Her strength, if it was returning at all, was doing so very slowly, and it was some weeks before she was allowed to leave hospital and return home, with strict instructions that she was still to be treated as convalescent, with regular visits to the outpatients department, and occasional longer ones for observation and tests.

It had been expected that in this way she would gradually recover her full strength. But this was what did not happen. She felt no pain and only occasional discomfort, but the weakness continued without abatement. Even to move from one room to another was a formidable effort. She never complained. Leo sometimes wished she would. He could carry cheerfully enough the extra burdens her incapacity laid on him; in a way he was glad of them, for they had the effect of drawing them together. What troubled him so deeply was her unvarying listlessness. Try as he might, rack his brains as he would for likely topics, nothing seemed to stimulate any response in her. She would merely say 'yes' or 'no', or 'I see' — just enough to show that she had been listening and had probably understood what he was saying, but she never added any observation of her own, never initiated anything at all.

The least unsuccessful — and that was not saying much — of his efforts to arouse her, showed when he kept her informed, as he did from time to time, of the consequences that were following the incident that had brought her down. These were not immediately spectacular, but he could tell her that they were definitely at work. The evidence that she and her friends had obtained was now incontrovertible; but the question was, what to do with it. She listened attentively, and sometimes with just a hint of the old eagerness, when he told her of the first step her friends in the group had decided on, their conference with the local member of parliament. Then there was the decision not to raise again at this stage the wider issue of the dump and its ominous contents, but to concentrate exclusively on the unlawful extraction and disposal of some of those contents that was proved to have been going on. Then again the preparation of the evidence and its despatch to the Director of Public Prosecutions. At last, after a long wait came the actual service of a summons on the manufacturers. This broke the silence that had hitherto prevailed and brought the media into it. There were paragraphs in the press that he could read to her, broadcast comments that he could persuade her to listen to; but still not a great deal; for the matter was now *sub judice* and any sensational or trenchant comment might amount to contempt of court. Then at last the trial itself, which was fully reported, though still with a minimum of comment for the same reason. At last, after a hearing that lasted several days, came the Judge's summing up, the jury's verdict of guilty on all charges and the sentence.

From the manufacturers' point of view, this was not very disastrous, since the most they could be convicted of was infringement of a certain restrictive clause in the legislation that had brought the dump into being, and the maximum fine for it was one they could easily afford. All the same it was when Leo read out to her certain *obiter dicta* the Judge had let fall while pronouncing sentence that Vi had shown something more like real interest than anything he had hitherto managed to evoke. "I cannot forbear adding," his lordship had said, "that, while the legal offence of which the defendants have been found guilty is limited to the unlawful removal of toxic material, there was here a totally callous disregard of their inevitable effects on innocent fellow human beings, in this case the inhabitants of a distant land, uneducated, unsuspicious and unprotected even by such half-hearted warnings as our own legislature has in its wisdom thought fit to erect. The circumstances of those removals, and above all of their destination, makes them comparable in abomination with the organised distribution of malignant drugs. It is fortunate for the defendants that the penalties exacted by the law bear so little relation to the offence."

And yet — what did it all amount to? That was the question that more and more haunted Vi during those interminable hours of inactivity that her disease was imposing on her. (For a disease it must be, though no specialist — and Leo had called in more than one — had succeeded in diagnosing it.) It was true that the public indignation the case had aroused had solved the immediate problem. For obvious reasons there would be no more surreptitious exports of that particular poison to the third world. More than that, the attention that had been called to the dump, as it became a news item, must mean the final suppression of the product. Everyone agreed, and the government did not attempt to dispute, that the pigeon-holed Inquiry would be pigeon-holed no longer, and everyone agreed that it must come down against any further manufacture. And yet, once more, what did it amount to? One tiny ingredient in the venomous mix of uncomprehended matter and empty or deluded mind that was threatening mankind and the earth itself had been neutralised, one cluster-bomb out of the mass that carpeted the target had been defused. That was how she saw it. Vague shadow-pictures of huge social structures, whether totalitarian states or multi-national corporations, not so much haunted as crushed her animal spirits. More and more impregnable, because more and more globally organised. And round what principle? Not the 'life' that maintains natural organisms in being with the help of death, its polar twin, not even an imagined abstract 'life-force'. Round an empty idea called 'growth' that now ruled all speculation and all planning, an Eleventh Commandment that had wormed into the Stone Tablets and, one by one, was steadily obliterating the other Ten: 'Thou shalt increase and multiply the total of material goods and services.' It was useless. She herself and those like her were attacking a giant with a pea-shooter, an armoured giant, secure therefore even against far more powerful missiles than theirs. They were dreaming that it is possible to wound the invulnerable.

To herself this hopeless depression felt more like *op*pression — oppression by the weight of a giant on top of her. Whatever it was, it lasted for several weeks, all the while settling more uninterruptedly down. She might never have emerged from it, had not Leo, clutching at a straw, had the notion that visitors might be good for her. That is to say, the right visitors, if only he could hit on them. She had of course been visited by a neighbour or two, by Jennifer, and by a few of her other friends in the group. But they had not managed to lift her burden. Now, as the result of Leo's initiative, two older friends came to see her. Harry Coppard's visit was followed only two days later by Herapath's, and with each of them she had had a long talk.

It was a few days after this second visit that the depression began to lift a little. Both of them, by what they had said, and Herapath explicitly, had encouraged her towards an indulgence which she had been sedulously denying herself, that of introspection. She began asking herself questions about herself. Had she perhaps been wrong in attaching such overweening importance, as against other things in her life, to her puny *deeds*? Had she cherished an exaggerated idea of *their* importance? It was Harry who had suggested to her that her thinking was too short-dated. He himself was under no illusion that his own life's work would be instrumental in changing the mental climate before the end of the century, or that, if it should change, that that life's work would have been of major importance in bringing the change about. "The Spring comes slowly up this way," he had quoted with a smile. Was it perhaps even a little arrogant, this obsession, this notion that she, Virginia Brook, had either succeeded, or

had failed to arrest the Gadarene decline of Western
civilisation? She could do, and she had done, *something*.
Oughtn't that to be enough?

Then Herapath had pushed her reflection deeper. It
was his visit, things he had said, that encouraged her to
review, not just what she had done, or failed to do, but also
what she *was*; what she had been in herself and among
those round her — as a daughter, as a wife, and, yes, as a
student, recovering in herself some of the past life of
humanity. She tried, and with some success, to see Virginia
Brook as a tiny cell in the real Organism, the only one in
the last resort that mattered, the evolving Spirit of
Humanity.

Thus, while the ebbing tide of her physical strength still
failed to turn, her spirits improved. She began to chafe at
inactivity instead of listlessly accepting it. What, in her
present circumstances, could she do? It was at this point
that she recalled something she had almost forgotten: that
book she had once intended to write. Was it relevant?
Writing was, after all, a kind of doing. The idea took
firmer and firmer hold of her. She could, she *would*, write
something. But what? Certainly nothing that involved
research, visits to libraries, heavy reading. Everything,
then, pointed to fiction of some sort. A novel? She had
not the strength, nor probably the faculty of invention it
demanded. But something shorter she might manage. A
Märchen? That was what she finally settled on, only she
decided to call it a *Conte*, preferring the old Romance label
for the genre, with which her studies had made her
familiar, to the later Romantic one.

SIX WEEKS LATER, on a warm August evening, husband
and wife were seated together in Vi's bedroom, awaiting
the arrival of the doctor. She was resting, fully dressed,
on her bed.

"Leo," she said suddenly, "I'd rather like you to read
that thing I've been writing. It's in the top drawer here."

"Rather!" he said, and added, not quite truthfully, "I've
been waiting for you to say that." He took the manuscript
out of the drawer. "I shall start as soon as we've got rid of
the Doctor," he said.

Vi's doctor — a circumstance unusual since the
introduction of National Health — had become
something approaching a friend of the family. Two days
earlier Leo had had an anxious talk with him, asking in
particular if any sort of prognosis was yet possible. The
doctor had shaken his head, but then had added: "I can
tell you what is my guess, if you like. No more than a
guess, but Merton (the name of the specialist) agrees with
it. It's – "

"Don't tell me," Leo interrupted. "Tell us both
together. Whatever it is, she's the kind who will want to
know it." And he had thereupon made the appointment
which was now about to be kept.

There was a knock at the door and Leo, picking up the
manuscript as he went, answered it, while Vi got up and
went into the sitting room, where three armchairs and a
tray with sherry on it were set waiting. She was followed
by Leo, who put the manuscript down on a side table
before he offered the doctor a chair and poured sherry for
the three of them. The doctor took a sip or two.

"As I told Leo," he began, "I can't tell you much more than you know already."

"We'd like to know all there is to know," said Leo.

"It would get very technical. I could tell you, for instance, that the histolysis done by the blood people in Vi's and similar cases shows a deficiency of iron atoms in the haemoglobin; but I doubt if it would mean much to you."

"And there's no way of remedying the deficiency?"

"Not until we've found the cause of it."

This was the only point at which Vi joined in the exchange. "Haven't there been cases where the discovery of an unexpected remedy came first?" she said.

"You mean because it forced people to ask *why* it should be a remedy?"

"Yes. I thought penicillin came in that way."

"Mm," said the doctor. "Well, nothing like that has happened here. I wish to heaven it would."

All three were silent for a few moments, and then: "The long and the short of it is," resumed the doctor, "that we are very much in the dark. The most we can do is to put together the two kinds of data that are all we have to go on, and see what they suggest. The first is of course the results of the tests, scanning and analyses and so forth, which have not been as informative as we would have liked. But at least they have enabled us to *rule out* quite a few unpleasant possibilities. When it comes to what should be *ruled in*, it's another matter. We still don't know exactly what it is we are dealing with. So we have to turn to the other kind, namely any available records of similar, or apparently similar, cases. You won't want me to give you details of these. You want me to be as definite as I can about the – " he looked at Leo a little uneasily — "about the prospects. All I can really say is, that Merton and I are of the same mind and we would have to put it this way. Vi's complaint is not definitively terminal. She could continue as she is now for an indefinite period, her condition could deteriorate, or it could improve. It is not impossible that she should recover altogether. On the other hand, a comparison of her symptoms with those in similar cases, indicates that her condition is definitely precarious. A change for the worse could come with little or no warning — and in that case the worse might quickly become the worst. I know you wanted me to be frank."

Vi nodded. There did not seem much to be said. But the doctor did find other things to say. Instancing one or two of the comparable cases that comprised his second class of data, he skilfully led the conversation to a more general and, with that, a deeper level; from his own experiences with incurable patients, to the behaviour of human beings in the face of death and even from that to speculations on the meaning, or meaninglessness, of life.

Vi, with one part of her, was listening and even occasionally joining in, but with another part of her she was elsewhere. While they were talking, the sun had been setting and she had been watching, through the window, the evening sky, where a few level streaks of cloud still glowed pink near the horizon, but all above them was one wide expanse of fathomlessly tender blue. She found it recalling to her memory another picture that had especially impressed her during her time in Italy. She had seen many pictures of the Madonna, but none quite like that one, where the outstretched arms were holding wide the blue cloak, as if to receive into its curve the whole of suffering humanity. It was almost with a start that she realised the doctor was on his feet and saying goodbye.

When Leo came back from showing him out, neither of them was disposed to comment on what he had told them. "We'll talk of it another time," Leo said. "Now you'd better get to bed." And, picking up the manuscript with a smile: "I've got work to do!"

Vi LAY IN bed, thinking. She was no longer depressed. Why was she no longer depressed, she asked herself. There was enough, surely, in what she had just heard, to depress anyone and with justification. To her surprise she realised that what had finally lifted her depression was the fact that the *Conte* had, well, 'come out of her'. Was that how you felt, when you had been delivered of a child, she wondered — relaxed? She recalled their agreement, years back, to defer any notion of raising a family 'at all events for the time being'. Was that a mistake? It didn't seem to matter. Something had come out of her, something that had form, and therefore had its own life. Had it got form — or was it an amateurish effort full of all sorts of crudities? What would people think of it if it were ever read by anyone besides Leo? Why wonder about that? She would probably never know anyway.

What was all that the doctor had been saying? Oh yes, and that didn't seem to matter so very much either. She might be going to die soon — or she might not. Why didn't it matter? Because she knew quite well that she, the one they called Virginia Brook just now, was a single cell in that vast Organism, had been one long before she was born and would still be one after her death; and, yes, that was why she had never managed to feel quite at home in a Church service, preoccupied as it assumed her to be with the salvation tomorrow of her own half-baked soul. "Growth!" It can never become form unless it is regulated by deaths. Otherwise proliferation, riot, anarchy. The trouble about that vast Organism was that each cell had a will of its own. That was what happened in cancer; cells took off on their own. Destroying form instead of creating it ... cells taking off on their own ... "All we like sheep ..." in the Plastics Age now, but it was the Iron Age that had led to it ... begun it all ... begun everything, including the change over from myth to allegory.

In the adjoining room Leo was still reading, as she drifted into unconsciousness.

VIRGINIA'S CONTE

THERE WERE THREE sisters living in a lonely cottage in a clearing in the woods. Exactly when does not matter, but it was a long time ago. Sometimes they got on very well together, sometimes not so well. If anything like a dispute or a quarrel arose between them, it would mostly be between one of the two elders and their younger sister Maria, or perhaps between both of them and Maria; for Gertrude and Agnes were never able to forget that Maria had been their father's favourite.

He was dead now, this father of theirs. But while he lived, he had become an increasingly wealthy man. A simple farmer to begin with, he lived at a time when the demand for iron, for agricultural implements, weapons of war and other purposes, was growing rapidly; and he had soon discovered that his own farm and the land surrounding it was rich in iron ore. So he had begun extracting and smelting it, at first in a small way and then, as time went on, had acquired more and more of the neighbouring land and gradually built up a flourishing industry. Yet he was not primarily interested in making money, and it was perhaps for that reason that upon his death he had been able to leave his three daughters only the cottage upon a sufficient holding of land, lying in a pleasantly wooded hollow, with enough coming in in rents to enable them to live there — if not in affluence at least in comfort.

But Maria's father had been something more than a farmer and later on an ironmaster. He was a thoughtful man with an enquiring mind and even, as time went on and his leisure increased, a diligent reader. As to the books he studied, they were a haphazard collection and not very numerous; for it was a time when books were few and hard to come by. Mainly they were concerned in one way or another with man's relation to God. But it was also a time when the principles and the dreams of alchemy were finding their way directly or indirectly into books on that and almost all other subjects. He followed, as best he could, where they led, with deep interest and some perplexity. One thing troubled him a good deal, since it interfered with his own dreams and convictions, and that was the place accorded to the metal, iron, in the philosophy of the alchemists. They called it "base" and "impure", and this made him uneasy. For he had his own dreams too.

He had lost Maria's mother at about the time when Maria herself was entering womanhood and, as time passed, his youngest daughter, so different from her two sisters, became his confidante. He was surprised to find how willing she was to listen to his private vision of a future world, in which iron would play an increasingly prominent part. It was not just a matter of spades and ploughshares, he would point out, and he told her of the huge difference it had made when men had first begun to fix iron tires to the wheels of their carts and wagons. Yet that, he was sure, was only the tiniest beginning. There would be vehicles made entirely of iron, perhaps even man-made iron horses to draw them. He foresaw a world, no doubt in a far distant future, when iron would be permeating and strengthening every detail of man's intercourse with nature. Sometimes, as she sat and listened, Maria would notice how his eyes lit up when he spoke of these things, almost as if, when he thought he was speaking of iron, he was really speaking of the strength and energy and courage latent in himself, only part of which had found expression in his outwardly successful life.

Not that she put it in that way to herself. Indeed she did not understand all he said. But she used to listen, and was glad to do so. For she was by nature a good listener. More than that, listening for her was not just a passive receiving; it was an active *noticing* of the person — or it might be, not a person, but a songbird or a gurgling stream that she was listening to. And if you are really noticing something, what you are noticing does not simply hit you, it enters into you. It was in this way that Maria listened — and listened. But all that had come to an end when her father died and the farmhouse, enlarged by then into a modest yeoman's mansion, passed into the hands of the new ironmaster who purchased the business.

It was some four years after his death when the three sisters were sitting together in their cottage one evening soon after nightfall. "What is that?" said Agnes, "I thought I heard shuffling footsteps."

They listened in silence, and sure enough someone or something appeared to be dragging its way towards the outer door. The shuffling noise stopped, and was followed by a faint knock on the door. For a moment they looked at each other with surprise and fear on their faces. Then Gertrude, the eldest, drew herself up and said proudly:

"We must go to the door and see who it is. Our father was the protector of all the lesser folk around him and we are his daughters."

[margin note: active listening - consciousness]

"Of course we must go," said Agnes. "We can put the chain up while we talk to whoever it is."

Maria said nothing, listening for any further sounds that might come from outside. Her two sisters went to the door and Agnes fastened the chain that allowed it to open wide enough to see and speak through, but not enough to admit anyone. They unlocked and opened the door and, standing outside it, beheld in the dim light from the interior, an extraordinary figure. It was a man of medium height, dressed in a mode they had never seen before. Or so he must once have been dressed, but his apparel from head to foot was so tattered and bedraggled that it was a marvel it was still holding together. What was even more noticeable was the extreme pallor of his weather-beaten face, which not even its deeply sunburnt skin could conceal. It was clear that he was at the end of his tether and could only just manage to keep standing. Nevertheless, as soon as the door opened, he made a feeble attempt at a ceremonious bow, as he addressed them in a language unknown to them. Receiving no answer but a doubtful stare, he tried again in another tongue, one which again they did not understand. In desperation he drew on his limited stock of English, murmuring in a voice so weak as to be barely audible, and with pauses to recover his breath: "Fair courteous ladies ... seeck man ... allow him rest?"

Agnes unfastened the chain. If she had a sharp tongue she also had a quick wit for practical decisions. But their visitor had hardly crossed the threshold before his legs gave way and he fell on the floor at their feet. He lay there without moving, unconscious. They looked at each other in consternation. Then Agnes turned to Maria, who had come out of the room and was standing behind them.

"Fetch some water from the well," she said, and Maria hurried out of the house, drew up a bucket of water and filled the pitcher she had brought with her. Meanwhile the visitor had recovered consciousness and opened his eyes, but was still too weak to move or speak. Gertrude bent down and with some difficulty unstrapped the large and curiously shaped pack he had been carrying on his shoulders. As she laid it aside, she was surprised to find that it was not nearly as heavy as its bulky appearance suggested. Then between them, half supporting, half dragging him, the two sisters got him onto a couch. Maria returned with the pitcher and Gertrude dipped her fingers in and dashed a little water over his face. This appeared to revive him slightly, but he made no attempt to speak. Instead, he opened his mouth and pointed into it.

"He's thirsty," cried Maria. "I believe he's dying of thirst." She ran forward as she spoke and, raising his head from the cushion with one arm, held the pitcher to his lips. He took a long draught, sank back with a sigh and closed his eyes. Deciding not to disturb his rest, they returned to their living-room. From time to time one of them came back to see if he was awake, and more than two hours had elapsed before that happened. Then they brought him a bowl of soup, which Maria had heated in readiness, and were glad to watch him eagerly drinking it.

But what to do next? He was obviously too exhausted to sustain the burden of question and answer in a strange tongue. It was clear that what he chiefly wanted was to go to sleep again.

"Perhaps," said Gertrude at last, "there may be something in his pack that would give us some notion of who he is and where he comes from." It had been brought into the room where he lay, and now she lifted it up and, with an enquiring glance in his direction, made as if to begin unfastening the flap. The visitor's response to her gesture was an enigmatic one. With a very slight smile — was it an apologetic smile? — he shook his head and pointed to himself:

"Trovatore," he said.

DURING THE NEXT few months the lives of the three sisters took on a new colouring. The apothecary for whom they sent on the following morning shook his head after a brief examination and advised them to consult an old and learned Doctor of Medicine, who lived not far off and had been a friend of their father's. The latter's verdict, after making sundry curious tests, was that the man was in the grip of a very severe, though not a contagious distemper, which he named with two Latin words. The patient would recover his strength in due course, he said, but when they asked him how long it would take, he refused to be more definite than "a long time". They decided thereupon that they had no choice but to continue accommodating and caring for him.

This showed itself to be all the more necessary, the more they learnt about him. Slowly, as the days passed — and it is not necessary to detail the difficulties of communicating with an enfeebled creature who did not speak their language — slowly the following facts about their visitor became known to them. His name was Paolo; he was born in Italy, but he had no home there and no longer knew if any of his family were surviving. Indeed he had no home anywhere, for he spent his life wandering from one country to another. At last he had crossed to this country from France, because England lay between France and a certain Island where there were no snakes, whose name he had difficulty in pronouncing, but which he was very anxious to visit. When they tried to ask him if he had any trade or how he kept himself alive on his travels, they were not certain if he had understood them; for the only answer they got was that mysterious word 'Trovatore'.

If that was all they learned in the first few days, it was otherwise as time went on. Paolo was growing stronger, and it soon became evident that he had an active mind and one that was quick of apprehension. Gradually he became more and more familiar with the language of his hosts, and here the old Doctor was of great help. A friend of the family as well as their physician, and interested in their extraordinary lodger not only as a patient but as a human being, he took to dropping in from time to time and staying to converse with Paolo about many things. This was made easier by the fact that the learned Doctor knew some Italian and Paolo a little Latin, a language which was almost as familiar to the Doctor as his mother tongue.

By the time the days had lengthened out and spring was turning into summer, Paolo was convalescent, no longer confined to his room or even, when the weather was fine, to the house. While his legs were still too weak to carry him more than a few yards at a time, he loved to be out in the little garden round the cottage. The good doctor observed this and approved, for it accorded well with his notions of therapy. Doctor Gropewell loved his art and studied it deeply; in fact by inclination he was more of a philosopher than a practitioner. While he revered the acknowledged masters and learned all he could from them, he also read as widely as possible elsewhere; and he formed his own judgment of any idea presented to him, accepting or rejecting it on its merits, as he saw them, and not by the measure of its accord with the views of recognised authorities. "Even Master Galen," he used to say, "did not know everything." And then, if he was in the right company, he would add that, yes, Galen was an inexhaustible treasure-house of experience and knowledge concerning the four humours and the many different ways of treating their excesses and defects, but he never penetrated to the spirits underlying them, or sensed the close relation of the humours within the human frame to the four elements in the natural world outside it. That was why Galen had never really discovered the healing influences at work in nature herself, if we would only attend to them. It was these influences, particularly those from the spirits of the air, that Gropewell had in mind, when he advised Paolo, as his strength continued to increase, to spend as much time as possible "al fresco" and suggested to his hosts that they should encourage him by taking extended strolls about the neighbourhood. If they

The 4 humours

blood, yellow bile, black bile, phlegm

felt disposed sometimes to carry victuals with them and take their meal seated in some warm or some shady spot out of doors, so much the better.

So it came about that throughout the following summer the four of them held an arcadian existence of walking, sitting, reclining, conversing, with grass underfoot, foliage overhead, and bird song in the air about them. Naturally it was Paolo who did most of the talking, in his Italianate but less and less halting English. He even gesticulated occasionally, as he was accustomed to doing when at ease in his own language. He had so much more to tell them. He had seen so much more of the world. And so he gave them in effect the story of his life — not of course coherently and in systematic order, but in snatches as it came to him. But the three sisters soon formed the habit of piecing together the snatches later on when they were alone together; and the story, so reconstructed, was roughly as follows:

Through some influence which his father, a merchant of some standing, had been able to exert, he was received in adolescence into the household of a princely family dwelling in a castle near to his birthplace, not in a menial capacity but with the status of a page. In recounting what followed, Paolo had some difficulty in explaining to his audience that far from there being some outstanding abnormality in his behaviour he was only doing what was practically expected of him in those circumstances. The lady of the castle was young and beautiful and some twenty years younger than her swarthy husband, the Count, who spent most of his time abroad either hunting or fighting with his noble neighbours. Paolo himself was more inclined towards literature and the arts (the future originally planned for him had been a career in the Church), and he soon began composing love-songs and singing them to his exalted mistress. His hearers were startled when he reached this part of his story, but when Agnes enquired if the Count had not become justifiably jealous, he only laughed. She was so far above him in rank, he tried to explain, that it was almost as if the songs were addressed to a being in another and better world.

Long before this the surprising size and shape of the pack Paolo had had with him when he arrived had ceased to be a mystery. Its contents included a small lute. So now he suggested that he could best show what he meant by singing one of his songs to them. When the last lute-string had ceased vibrating, he did his best to translate the words of the song into English. They were to the effect that the singer was dying of despair because of his hopeless but unquenchable love, and then (in the final stanza) that this very despair was more highly prized by him than all the gold in the bed of Pactolus. Agnes said nothing. Gertrude, in no uncertain terms, voiced her contempt for such unmanly self-abasement. Maria asked him to sing it again.

After that, it became the normal practice for the Trovatore to carry his lute with him on their excursions, so that music was added to conversation in their enjoyment of those summer days. Not all his songs were in the mode that Gertrude had found objectionable, and many of them, besides being tunefully pleasant, were helpful in bringing alive a point he had reached in the story of his life. He told them how, after a time he had had to leave the castle, owing to some change of circumstances, how by that time he had become enchanted by his own music almost as much as by the Contessa, so that music had become a way of life for him, and he had decided to live as a Trovatore, a wandering singer. There were others in the same way of life with whom he associated from time to time. It would take too long to detail the account he gave of these, but they seemed to be of three different kinds. First there were the Giullari, or Giullari d'amore. Fortunately or unfortunately not all the ladies a Trovatore serenaded were as inaccessible as Paolo's Countess. A Giullare sang of successful as well as unsuccessful love-affairs and not only of love-affairs, but also of the beauties of spring and summer and of the joys of drinking and good company; and there were drabs in plenty who mocked their songs but served them well enough in other ways.

Then there were the religious, whom some called the Giullari di Dio, and with whom Paolo clearly felt more in sympathy. Their inspiration was not some high-born lady but the misery of the poor and the wickedness of the great bulk of mankind. Here he found it necessary to sketch in to some extent the background to their songs, and in particular he horrified the sisters with his description of the Disciplinati, as they were called, and their response to the call for repentance that was going out from those of the Franciscan persuasion: the long lines of penitent sinners parading through the streets and villages, each man savagely whipping the bare back of the man in front of him as they went singing their misereres. The verses of those who were moved by such scenes and what lay behind them, were in the same measures, often sung to the same tunes, as the Trovatori used, but with a very different subject matter. Different in all respects but one. There was one link between them and their opposite numbers, namely, the dream of a lady. Only, if a lady was involved, and she often was, it was always Mary the Mother of God, her sorrows for her suffering Son and her compassion for the wicked, the weary and the oppressed. Of these Paolo began speaking with deep respect, but then checked himself and relapsed into silence, an uneasy silence as if he were struggling to find his own meaning and how to express it. At last, "Not my way ..." he said, staring straight in front of him, and, after a pause, "Men not angels ..." Another pause, and then with great emphasis, "*Music!*" finally after a still longer pause, and with still greater emphasis: "And to *fight* bad thing."

The third class, to which Paolo himself belonged, lay somewhere between the other two. He called them the *fedeli d'Amore*, or faithful servants of Love, and he was distressed because as more and more of them defected either to the one side or to the other, he felt they were a diminishing company. That was the reason why he had wandered farther and farther abroad, hoping he might find that somewhere in the world *fedelità d'amore* was still the guiding star. First of all to the South of France, the old Roman Provincia, where he had spent many months and had found much to admire. Some of their songs were sweeter than any he had heard in his own country. But as time went on, he became dissatisfied. Among the

collective unconscious

troubadours, as they were called in that part of the world, there was already too great a preponderance of the first class, too many giullari, or jongleurs, content to sing of light o' loves, their equals in rank, or of the joys of the wine cup.

So he had passed on to High Germany, where he had heard there were those called Minnesinger, among whom the old tradition was better preserved. That was partly true, he found, when at last he arrived there, but not true enough to satisfy him for long. Thus, he had been led to ponder more and more deeply on the mysterious relation between spirit and flesh, and to seek more and more eagerly for the dwelling-place on earth of the true way, the Trovatore way, of handling it.

Where was that way to be found at its best? Where for instance had it originated? And now he learned from some of the better educated among his fellow craftsmen a fact of which he had already heard a rumour in his own country, but to which he had paid little attention. The Emperor's court in Sicily, was a strange place where nobles and lesser men from many countries met together. It had been found that several of the song-modes most in favour among the troubadours, the length and arrangements of the lines and the distribution of their rhymes, were borrowed from songs already traditional in a foreign language. Scholar-poets from Spain, and others from the East, had brought them there, dark-skinned men not of the Christian faith, intermingling with the denizens of Italy and Provence — not of the Christian faith and, perhaps for that very reason less ready to substitute a pale waxen idol for a flesh-and-blood *inamorata*.

And yet, Paolo had heard how it was from a leading position in that very Court that the famous Fra Pacifico had come back to join Fra Francisco and become one of his twelve disciples.

He had determined to make his way to Sicily and find things out for himself and was on the point of starting when something occurred to make him hesitate. He had made friends with a devout and learned Frenchman, one of the many followers of Peter Waldo, who had fled to Germany from persecution by the Church for heresy. This old man had taught him many things — things it would take long to describe. He had even suggested that God had ordained him, Paolo, to become a Trovatore in order gradually to teach others.

Paolo paused there. To teach them what? the sisters asked. And he made the curious answer: "To see things other men cannot see, things that are seen only with inside eyes, not at all with outside ones." Paolo had sought his aged friend's advice on his own growing perplexities and, while discussing these, had learned from him that Ireland, not Rome, was the source from which the Christian faith had first been carried into Europe. That was several centuries ago. But from all he had heard, the old man said, and unless the original inspiration had sadly faded, a judicious traveller would come nearer there than anywhere else to the Wellspring from which flowed a true understanding of the relation between Spirit and flesh. The whole manner in which this man spoke had impressed Paolo deeply. For a time he had wavered, unable to make up his mind between Sicily and Ireland, but in the end he had decided for Ireland and, as his hearers knew, was on the way there when he collapsed on their doorstep.

IT WAS STILL early afternoon on the day when Paolo reached this point in his narrative, and the four of them fell silent. There was a feeling that further conversation would be something of an anticlimax. In the end Agnes and Gertrude decided to return home, leaving Maria and Paolo to round off the day with a *spatiare*, as the latter called it, an extensive stroll through the neighbourhood. They made their way towards the further slope of the hollow in which the house was situated and, as the ground began to rise, came upon a rivulet of clear water that issued from the turf in a bubbling spring. They paused there and both of them cupped their hands and drank from it. They stood still to survey the spot, almost a meadow, at which they had arrived. The grass there seemed greener than the turf they had been walking on, the flowers richer in size and colour and more crowded. After a few moments Maria made as if to move on, but Paolo held up his hand and remained standing. Maria looked at him curiously. Was he in some kind of trance? Certainly he was deeply moved. To break the awkward silence, "Isn't it beautiful?" she said.

At first he did not answer. Then, stirring himself a little, "Yes indeed, but also more than beautiful." Maria observed him still more curiously.

"Can you explain in what way?"

"I do not know enough English words. How do you say

— sacral? sacred?" Maria's curiosity changed to surprise.

"It is strange you should say that," she said, and went on to tell him of a local custom, by which the country folk from many miles around assembled at the spring with their families on the first day of May. First the children strewed flowers and wreaths in a loose circle around the spring, and then, together with their parents and all who were not too old for it, they danced round it to the notes of a pipe and the beat of a tabor. The tunes and the dances, some gay and some solemn, remained the same year after year, but the people never seemed to tire of them.

pagan worship

"That is why this particular spot is called *The Dance Ground*," she told him. And he nodded rather as if it was just what he had been expecting to hear.

"How is it that you *knew*?" she said, as they walked on.

At first he did not answer, and she wondered if he was going to. But at last, "Perhaps," he said slowly, "… in a way … I have already told you that."

collective unconscious

Maria checked herself from an impatient question, leaving him to explain himself or not, as he thought fit. He did think fit. They were walking now through a grove of oak and beech and birch trees, and Paolo, speaking slowly and thoughtfully, tried to explain to her how a true Trovatore, a faithful one, becomes able, as time goes on, to see things that others do not see. He learns, to start with, by seeing things — oh so many things — that others do not see at all, although they are there, yes, in one person, in one lady who is his *inamorata*. He paused and laid his hand on her arm to indicate that he wished them to cease walking. They stood facing one another; as Maria, her eyes on the ground, asked him:

"How do you know they are really there? Are you sure they are not – " But he held up his hand to stop her.

"I know what you wish to say. And I could answer it, but it would be difficult in your language, or even in mine." And he seemed at first to be talking to himself rather than to her, as he went on:

"It was the old man, the Vaudois, who explained it best. How each one of us, not only beautiful ladies …" he hesitated, and she felt he had been on the point of adding "like yourself," but he went on "… is not only a visible body, but also a whole invisible world. Only we are blind — blind to each other and to ourselves. But how can I expect you to understand?"

Maria raised her eyes, and they looked at one another for a long moment in silence. At last, "Perhaps I do understand," she said, "perhaps you need not say any more." He made her a low bow, so low that it was almost a reflex action when she held out her hand to be kissed; and from now on there was an understanding between them that was more than doctrinal.

They were near the end of the path through the woodland and now, as they emerged from it, had only the clear sky above and a wide prospect before them; wide rather than deep, for they had reached the top of the ridge, and though the ground dipped in front of them, less than a mile away it rose to another ridge of nearly the same height as their own. They stood gazing with satisfaction over the expanse of gorse and heather, until they noticed that the sky beyond the second ridge was far

[handwritten margin note: each person is) connection to ⎫ mythopoeia / more than a ⎭ body]

from clear. It was not exactly a cloud, more something like a veil of smoke that was rising from behind it, and it must have been light breezes that were coiling it into obscurely fantastic shapes. Maria would have drawn Paolo's attention to them, but before she could do so, he uttered a sharp exclamation and asked her what the smoke was coming from. She told him that the valley beyond the ridge was very different from the one before them. It was crowded with the fires of charcoal-burners. He asked her what charcoal was and, when she had explained, enquired further what it was used for. "For making iron," she replied, and she told him how the ground they were standing on, and indeed the whole of the heath, was rich in iron ore, especially rich in some parts, poorer in others. She added that the smoke they saw came not only from the fires of the charcoal-burners, perhaps not mainly from them, but also from furnaces in which the ore was being purified into metal. He seemed only half interested in these details, and for a time they continued gazing in silence. At last, "How strange it all looks!" she murmured.

"Strange? But tell me, do you not see the Shape?"

"My fancy sees many shapes, now one and now another."

"I see *one* Shape. I see Wings and — a Countenance."

She looked a question, but for a moment or two he remained silent. Then:

"Lady Maria," he said, "it is not only the good things, unseen by others, that a humble Trovatore learns to see. There are also bad things ..." He stopped short.

man's need for material wealth destroys ethereal beauty

"I am listening," said Maria in a low voice. But it seemed he had no more to say. So after a pause she took up the thread herself.

"Can you tell me," she asked, "what — what you meant when you said 'a countenance'? Did you mean something like a human face?"

"No," he replied, and then, "Yes — yes — not like, but the same. It might well be that I shall see a man's or a woman's face and I shall say to myself 'That is the face I saw above the ridge, in the smoke'."

"Surely not the *same!*"

"Oh Lady Maria, it is so difficult that I — what is your word? — I *shirk* trying to speak of it. And yet how I long to! How I long for myself and my lady to know the same thing! Listen, in the unseen world different things are not separate from one another like they are in the world we see with our outside eyes."

"Things?"

"Yes, or creatures — Beings."

So, as they retraced their steps, he struggled to tell her what he thought he knew about the Countenance he had seen in the smoke. It belonged to One who could not only possess, but for a time actually *become*, the human being he had chosen for his purpose. Only once did Maria interrupt him.

"You are speaking of the Devil, of Satan?"

"I am not learned in names," was his reply, "though I have heard more than one. The Jews speak of Baalzebul, the Persians, and some of the Vaudois, of Ahriman. Whatever he is called, Lady, he is the Enemy — the Bad One."

THEY WALKED THE rest of the way home in silence, an oppressive silence Maria felt it to be, though not because of any tension between them; rather the reverse. It stemmed from what they had spoken of, not from what they had left unspoken. As soon as they entered the house, they heard a man's voice in the living room. They looked at each other in surprise and stood listening for a while. A conversation was going on between the man — no, two men apparently — and the sisters.

Maria opened the door and went in followed by Paolo. The two visitors were not unknown to her. They were the Ironmaster Hugo and his Foreman-manager Godfrey. Paolo made as if to leave the room, but Maria stopped him. She simply said, "Don't go Paolo," and, though her sisters raised their eyebrows, they raised no objection. Hugo briefly explained to Maria what they had come about. It concerned the cottage they now lived in and the demesne in which it stood. Hugo himself had moved into the main residence after their father's death. He had decided, he said, that the time had come to expand his undertaking. For that he would need more land.

"I have been explaining to your sisters," he said, and he seemed a little embarrassed, "that your holding is ideal for the purpose." And he went on to repeat what he had just been saying before she and Paolo entered; namely, that he could offer them a house and land not far off, where they would be just as comfortable, or even more so, than they were at present. At this point Maria interrupted abruptly and bluntly. "Do you mean you want *all* our land?" she said. The Ironmaster hesitated. "Well, yes,"

Ironmaster wants to buy her land [handwritten marginal note] he said. "We — I — should need it all, and indeed would be glad of more if I could get it." The three sisters looked at each other, and shook their heads. There was an awkward silence, during which a picture arose in Maria's mind of the Dance Ground, not as she knew it, but with its flowers trampled or uprooted, with slovenly paths criss-crossing it between one unsightly erection and another, and with the rivulet from the spring no longer running clear but slimy with mud and grease, refuse and slag, and broadening here and there into a stagnant, blackening pond.

"What would you do with our land?" she asked.

"Well," he said, "you know what ironworks are like."

There was silence again. Hugo's embarrassment was evidently increasing; it even looked as though he was perspiring a little.

"But perhaps," he began, "if you – "

The Foreman, who up to now had said nothing, interrupted him.

"It is essential," he said, and, looking all the time hard at his employer but not addressing him, he went on:

"It is not just your situation, snugly adjoining our own. We have discovered that just this part of the subsoil is particularly rich in clay ironstone — easily workable ore."

Silence again, and again all three sisters shook their heads.

"We really must have it" said Godfrey. But now, though Agnes appeared to be weakening, Gertrude was roused. She was the oldest and entitled to speak for all three.

"We are very sorry to disappoint you," she said, "but

this is where our father meant us to live, and this is where we will go on living."

Hugo stirred in his chair as if he intended to give up and take his leave, but before he could rise to his feet, Godfrey threw at him abruptly: "Haven't you forgotten something?"

Now Hugo really was embarrassed and there really was a bead of perspiration on his forehead. In a halting way, and looking from time to time at his Foreman, he told them he had recently looked into the title deeds, which went back a long way into the past, and had discovered that the sisters' land had never been legally severed from his own and therefore still formed part of it. In fact it really belonged to him already. He had not wished to raise this point, or even to tell them, provided they agreed to his suggestion. But now, with their refusal, he — well, he really had no choice; and as he said this, he again looked at his Foreman. Was he soliciting the man's *approval*?

If so, he seemed to have earned it. For Godfrey nodded vehemently. "Absolutely essential," he said. And he went on in eager tones, addressing only Hugo, to enumerate some of the reasons for it. The exchange that followed between the two of them was largely unintelligible to the other occupants of the room, being much concerned with such things as bloomeries, furnaces, slag, slag-tapping, and hammer ponds. Finally it was Godfrey who turned to Gertrude and said,

"There are so many good reasons for it. The Master will have to have the land. And he means to have it."

To which Gertrude replied that she understood what

forceful destruction

had been said and would be looking elsewhere for help and advice.

"Will you not at least," said Hugo, "look well at the other fief I am offering you, and see if perhaps you like it better than a quarrel?"

Gertrude looked at her sisters and, when they nodded, agreed to do so.

"I shall make arrangements for it," said Godfrey. And with that the visitors took their leave.

There was silence in the room after they left; almost a stunned silence; until, if only because it must be broken somehow, Gertrude turned to Paolo and asked, "What do you think?"

He did not hesitate. "I say only, do not trust that man!" And Maria wondered at the meaning glance he gave her as he spoke.

The events that followed need not be narrated in detail. First there was Godfrey's second visit, alone this time, and ostensibly on business. He told them that Flint Cottage, the house Hugo was offering them in exchange for their own, was the one in which he himself was at present living; that, being an untidy bachelor, he wanted to put it in better order before they inspected it. Also he would have to seek out another dwelling for himself. As to what had been said last time, there was no great hurry. He was sorry if he had seemed to be abrupt. It might be a week or two before he would suggest their visit of inspection.

He seemed anxious to dispose of all this as briefly as possible, and it soon became apparent that he wished to create the atmosphere, not so much of a business interview as of a friendly visit between neighbours. He hoped, he said, that they would all remain friends whatever happened, and he looked round at them with an expression that was meant to be a smile but looked, to Maria at least, more like a scowl trying to turn into one. He made conversation, first on matters of local interest and then about themselves and their way of life. How did they all spend their time? He even ascertained that Maria liked being alone and that she was fond of walking or resting in a certain secluded part of the demesne. He asked politely about Paolo and was told something of his history and his dramatic appearance on their doorstep. Yes, he had dealings with foreigners himself. They were even employing one or two at the Ironworks — Frenchmen — Italians — he wished he was a scholar and knew their languages; for misunderstandings kept arising when he was giving them instructions or getting information from them. And so on, and so on, till at last with another smile all round and a good deal to the relief of his hosts — except for Agnes, who was drawn by his masculinity — he left them.

This visit was followed by a serious talk between Paolo and Maria. She asked him if he had noticed the way Agnes kept looking at the Foreman. No, what he *had* noticed was the way Godfrey kept looking at Maria herself. And it was only now he told her — for one thinks many times before speaking to another of what only the 'inside eyes' have seen — that the Foreman's face was the very Countenance he had seen in the smoke behind the ridge.

Two days later Maria, out on one of her solitary walks, was just entering the Dance Ground, when to her surprise she saw a figure approaching from the opposite direction. It was Godfrey. As soon as they were within speaking distance, he stopped and inclined his head in what he intended to be a bow. She stood still, and he came on and respectfully greeted her, enquiring whither she was bound. She told him she had no errand, had merely been enjoying a walk in the fresh air, and moreover that she had been about to turn back. He asked if he might accompany her a little way, and, as she felt she could not very well refuse, they were soon side by side. This time he made no attempt at desultory conversation, but reverted at once to his first visit to their house together with Hugo, and it was clear he was anxious to please her. He had felt, he said, that she was the one of the three who had the strongest objections to his — or rather Hugo's — proposal. Would she do him the favour of stating them more clearly? He doubted if she had realised all that was involved.

Maria cast about in her mind for any one of her many objections there might be some hope of his understanding. She did not know much of the details of the iron industry or the names of its different processes, but she did know that the house to which it was proposed they should move stood beside a hammer pond, and therefore within the perpetual noise from the hammering its waters powered. With this Godfrey made a feeble attempt to sympathise, but it was an attempt that failed. Before he knew what he was saying, he was carried away by his own enthusiasm.

Had she ever thought that noise meant life? As for

himself, he *liked* noise. He lived in it — or it lived in him. Not *all* noise of course, but this was rhythmic noise. He felt the rising and falling of the hammers and the music of the noise they made, in the beating of his own pulse, his own heart. There followed more to the same effect, but it was clear she was not responding. So he stopped abruptly, only adding: "And it will be the same with you, when you have lived there for a time." When she said only that she did not want it to be the same, he decided to leave it there for the time being and asked her if she had other objections.

Maria was not a lawyer, used to answering questions and arranging thoughts. She asked him instead whether it was not possible to use some neighbouring valley for his schemes instead of theirs. For a moment he was irritated, but he concealed it with a laugh. He stood still and spread out his arms in a gesture that seemed to embrace the whole landscape. Couldn't she see that they needed it *all*? This little valley was just the place for a much larger pond, which would feed the bloomeries in land still farther off and lower down. Again he forgot himself in his own enthusiasm.

"We shall change everything," he said, "and even all this is only a beginning. All this," with a wave of his hand, "is standing still — or even moving backward. The way is forward," and as he spoke he took a step forward, shifting his foot from the camomile tuft beneath it and planting it firmly on a spread of pimpernel. "Iron is the secret of the future of the world; it is an iron world man wants, not one of useless trees and pretty flowers. In fifty — perhaps a hundred years' time, all this will have disappeared. It will be an iron valley in an iron country."

He was speaking now almost as one possessed; and quite suddenly he seemed to realise it. He turned towards her and took hold of her hand. Maria, with her eyes on the ground, had indeed been listening, but she had also been thinking. She had been thinking of her father's enthusiasm for the magic metal and its future, and wondering why it did not help her to sympathize with her companion, as she had half sympathized with *him*. Why were the two enthusiasms so different? And then she remembered what Paolo had told her of his vision, and she raised her eyes.

She found him looking fixedly at her. No longer possessed, with his voice at a lower pitch and a different expression on his face, "And yet," he said, "and yet — I am human and can make sacrifices. I would even sacrifice my ambition for — for – " He stopped speaking, and it was as if he swallowed something. Then suddenly: "Maria, Maria, Maria, don't you see — you *must* see how I long for you — ever since that afternoon in your house — I *want* you — more than I want anything — you, you, *you*!"

She withdrew her hand and took a step backward, and with that he partly recovered himself. "I should have waited," he muttered, and then, more loudly:

"Do not be frightened, my dear. Let us go on talking. I am not so unreasonable. Nor, perhaps, are you."

And he made as if to walk on. Maria, on the point of dismissing him with disgust, recalled how much depended,

[margin handwritten note: Father loved the land + wanted it for his family. Iron master wants it for profit]

not only for herself but for her sisters, on this man's good will, and she reluctantly resumed her place at his side.

For what followed she was partly prepared by his outburst. It was simple enough. Although Hugo was his master, the relation between them was such that he would accept Godfrey's advice on anything to do with the business. Moreover the man was already uneasy at the prospect of turning the family out of their own house. If only she would give herself to him, Godfrey would see to it that they were left undisturbed.

Once again, and for the same reason, Maria checked her answer even as it reached her lips.

"Do you understand at all how much you are asking?" she said, "I — you — you must give me time."

For the rest of the short distance they walked on in silence. When they came in sight of the house, Godfrey turned to leave her. But first he asked her if she would be taking the same walk on the following day, and she nodded assent.

When she reached home, her mind in a turmoil, she said nothing to her sisters of what had occurred, but after a while she asked where Paolo was. They did not know. He had gone out soon after she left. They had hardly finished speaking, when he came in with a broad smile on his face. "You behold a workman!" he said. Of course they asked him what he meant, and it all came out. He had walked up to the Ironworks and boldly offered his services as an interpreter, first reminding Hugo of what had been said of their difficulties with some foreign labourers. The Ironmaster had hesitated. It was usually his Foreman

Godfrey who engaged and dismissed the workmen, and he was not sure — but yes, this time he would make the decision himself. So Paolo was engaged at a low wage, to be present when required as an interpreter and, when not so needed (which would be most of the time), to do any little jobs that required no special skill.

While they were all four together, Paolo gave as his reason his long-felt desire to be able to pay them at least something in exchange for their generous hospitality, especially as he would soon be well enough to resume his travels. Later, when he was able to speak to Maria alone, he told her his real reason. He wanted to find out more about Godfrey. No need to tell her why! In return she told him all that had just occurred between Godfrey and herself.

She had half expected an outburst of wrath, but instead Paolo only nodded his head, as though it was what he had half expected to hear. He was even glad she had responded so cautiously. And he told her why. He believed now that they were both together somehow appointed to detect and, if possible, expose some obscure but powerful evil that was threatened by, or through this man Godfrey. It was a long talk, for he was half ashamed of what he was asking her to do, if only she were strong enough. In the end it was settled, that, while Paolo learned all he could at the Ironworks, she would find some way of keeping Godfrey at arm's length while seeming to encourage him not to despair.

When she met Godfrey next day therefore, she told him she still had not made up her mind and that she must have at least a week in which to do so. And, with an angry frown, he agreed. Meanwhile Paolo, spending his days at the Ironworks, was learning something of what went on there, though not nearly as much about Godfrey as he could have wished. The Foreman, annoyed that he had been taken on by Hugo without reference to himself, had a grudge against him from the beginning. Not only did he rebuke him whenever possible, for the way he had performed a task, but he went out of his way to find excuses for insulting him, in the hearing of his fellows, for being a dirty foreigner. It was more like hatred than a mere grudge, and perhaps there was a deeper reason for it. Had he suspected that there was a relation between Paolo and Maria that was beyond and above his understanding?

Whatever it was, it effectually prevented Paolo from learning anything about his enemy by direct exchanges. It was otherwise with indirect ones. From his fellow labourers he soon learned something about what went on at the Ironworks, and much about Godfrey: for instance, that they all disliked him intensely and that the Master was completely under his thumb. Not only was it his orders, as Foreman, that they had to obey, but they knew very well that it was *his* decisions on general policy, not Hugo's, that guided the whole concern. With all that, they were also afraid of him, afraid of him not just as a hard taskmaster, but with a superstitious fear. There were strange rumours about him, and one in particular about which they were reluctant even to speak. Some months ago there had been a bad accident. A huge bar of iron had slipped and fallen to the ground, from a considerable height, crushing two men to death. But there had been a third man standing beside them — Godfrey. How was it he had escaped without even a trace of injury? Paolo gave no answer, but he drew his own conclusions.

Meanwhile other things had been happening. Gertrude had visited their father's man of affairs in the neighbouring town, and he had examined the title deeds to their land. Alas, it seemed that Hugo had been right. Someone had made a mistake. Though it was clearly not their father's intention, the crucial document was so worded that the ownership had passed to Hugo when he acquired the Ironworks. Moreover, since it concerned landed property the Court of Equity could not interfere and there was no hope of rectifying the error. They were at his mercy.

At about the same time Maria's stipulated week for reflection had expired. She had not given him either of the answers he expected. On the evening before the rendezvous, she had consulted with Paolo, whom she had now learned to trust absolutely, and he, out of the knowledge of men and women he had acquired during his vagabond existence, had given her certain advice. Desire plays strange tricks, he had said, even with bad men. So when she was with Godfrey the following day, she had not refused him. "I want more time," she had said, "more meetings like this." And when he flatly refused, she had looked at him long and earnestly with her lovely eyes wide open on his defences.

"I am learning to know you," she said. "In a little while I shall know you better still. Would you rather I gave myself unwillingly to an enemy who has me in his power, or — or gladly to a friend?"

Poor Godfrey! He was never to be nearer to heaven — or less distant from it — than at that moment. A rush of feeling brought him a glimpse of what he would miss by heavy-handedness. "How long?" was all he said, and there was pleading rather than menace in his voice. She felt on sure enough ground now to ask him not to insist on fixing a time limit, and when a shadow of suspicion crossed his face, she added casually: "Three — four weeks? I don't know."

THIS PRECARIOUS UNDERSTANDING between the two was something of an embarrassment when another occasion brought Godfrey and the three sisters together. A day had been fixed for the sisters to make their promised visit of inspection to Godfrey's cottage, which was to be their future home, and with little enough enthusiasm they set out on the expedition. A footpath from their own cottage led at first through a patch of woodland, where the trees were old and grand, with generous spaces between them. It was a spot the three of them visited in the spring of every year to enjoy the bluebells, the deep green leaves and pale stems clouded with a haze of blue differing from that of the sky above it only in the hyacinthine fragrance breathed by returning life. How much we have been taking for granted! thought Maria, as the heaviness of her heart at the thought of losing all this strengthened her private resolve to save it.

The path soon left the shelter of the trees and wound its way down a sloping field towards a stream, which it crossed by a footbridge. Thereafter it skirted the length of the hammer pond it was feeding, till it reached the dam at the opposite end. The ground fell sharply beyond the dam, and on the bottom of the hollow the Ironmaster had erected the most recent and most modern of his installations called Black Hollow Forge. Already, as the visitors approached the footbridge, they heard men's voices and the sounds of spade and pick-axe. Just below the bridge half a dozen men were at work cutting into the left bank of the stream. Godfrey himself was there directing the work and, when he saw them on the bridge, he hailed them and made his way up the bank.

"Good," he said, "I'll come with you. I've been waiting for you."

Gertrude asked him what the men were doing, and he said they were going to divert into this stream another fuller stream that approached it at this point, but at present only joined it much lower down. "Last summer," he said, "the water level in the pond fell too low. It slowed down production." Then, after a few sharply worded directions to the workmen, he joined the sisters on the bridge and led the way towards the dam. Up on the hillside they glimpsed the big house where they had lived when their father was alive, and where Hugo now dwelt. The smooth waters of the pond shone like a broad bright meadow and the scene would have been peaceful enough but for the rhythmic thud of the hammers from the Forge below the dam.

It was to this dam that the hammerpond owed its origin,

since it had been built to collect the water from a number of rills and streams that tended to converge at the point where it was constructed. There were two sluices underwater near the foot of the dam, by which the pressure of the outflow could be directed either on to the hammers beating the half-processed red-hot ore in the Forge, or out into the stream below. The former, Godfrey told them, was called the Workway and the latter the Freeway. The Freeway was only opened when the Forge was idle, which nowadays was very seldom — only for a short time in the small hours in fact — since one of the improvements he, Godfrey, had introduced into the Ironworks was a system of working in shifts.

They paused on the stout wooden planks that bridged the water, as it rushed out of the pond down the Workway under the road and into the Forge. The sisters were looking, not at the pond, but at the other side of the road, where there was a twenty-foot drop to the floor of the valley. Down there was the Forge — a massive rectangular building that rose three storeys high. The lower two storeys were below the level of the road, and a plank bridge spanned the ten-foot gap between the road and a door in the third storey. The building itself was black owing to the material used in its construction. Thousands of flints had been gathered and knapped to face the outer walls of the Forge, like a rich covering of glittering scales, and it was these that had given the place the name of Black Hollow Forge.

The work of the Forge was carried on in the two lower floors of the building. On the upper floor, whose windows,

dark and curtainless, looked out on to the road, Godfrey
proposed to live when he had vacated his cottage. "Most
of my gear is already in there," he said. "Only a few
necessaries left in Flint Cottage, where I am still sleeping.
You could move in next week."

"But the noise! How could you bear it?"

"Doesn't trouble me at all. On the contrary I like it. I
get a good deal of it, as it is, in Flint Cottage. You'll
probably get to like it yourselves. Come along, the cottage
is only a stone's throw away."

And then he led them on away from the dam and up a
little side road, where Flint Cottage stood overlooking
Black Hollow Forge. It was some slight comfort that the
cottage was placed not actually in the hollow but high
enough to be on a level with the pond. But the contrast
between it and their own beloved cottage was
overwhelming. Its walls were crusted with flints the same
as those on the Forge. A thimblefull of sunlight filtered in
through the upper windows. Standing inside with the
windows closed, they could still hear the thumping of the
hammers. A feeling of depression, almost of despair, crept
into Maria's breast and she thought she saw tears in
Gertrude's eyes.

The four of them stood silent for a while, and it was
clear that even Godfrey felt awkward and embarrassed.

At last: "Thank you," said Gertrude. "We have seen
all we came to see. Your Master will be hearing from us."

PAOLO KNOCKED ON the door of Flint Cottage. Work was over for the day, but Godfrey had bidden him to his house because there were "things they needed to talk about." He expected a string of complaints, perhaps a threat of dismissal. But Godfrey opened the door and invited him in with the nearest he could manage to a smile. He bade Paolo seat himself and produced two mugs which he filled from a cask of ale with a hand that Paolo noticed was inclined to tremble a little. Gradually it came out. He wanted to talk about Paolo himself, not as an employee, but as a friend of Maria's family and of Maria herself. He recalled his visit to their house and what he had heard there. Did not Paolo find it hard to live, here in England, the kind of life he was now living? So very different from the adventurous one the sisters had told of him. And so on and so on.

At first the Italian was puzzled. But he soon saw what it was that lay behind the forced friendliness. He was not unfamiliar with jealousy and its symptoms. So he was not surprised at the path into which Godfrey was tortuously guiding the conversation, especially as the painful effort the latter was making to control himself grew more and more apparent. No doubt Paolo was by now quite a member of the family? Was Godfrey right in thinking that there was perhaps a special understanding between Paolo and the youngest sister? Why should he think that? Well, he had sometimes seen them together. Probably they had found they had a good deal in common. Was he right? "Yes," said Paolo, "we both love music and we both love flowers and, yes, and running water." For some reason this reply exasperated Godfrey so unbearably that he dropped the mask and became his genuine sneering self.

"Music! Flowers! You've forgotten one thing, haven't you? Love!" In Paolo's breast a head of anger was building up and steadily increasing its pressure, and he was as steadily holding it down — a dangerous thing for a Southerner to do. He remained silent, as Godfrey blundered confusedly on. Wasn't it true that Paolo had spent his whole life making love to women? Music, Poetry, Flowers — oh yes, but that was what it all meant. Things of the past all of them, except love. A relic of the past, that was what Paolo was. If he could peep into the future of his flowers and his running water and his music, he would have the surprise of his life. And as to that "understanding", would Paolo like to know that *he* had an understanding with Maria too? Had had for some time now. Only perhaps *his* understanding of what is meant by 'an understanding' — what is meant by this 'love' Paolo was forever singing about (so *he* had been told) — was rather different. *His* understanding of Maria was what she looked like with her clothes off. Should he tell him about it — in detail?

By now Paolo's concealed anger had reached boiling point. Indeed it had turned to fury. Not that he was deceived by that dirty lie; he would still have kept it down, simply because so much more was at stake than his private quarrel with the monster before him. He would have kept it down, if Godfrey had not made his final remark:

"In short, Paolo — and this is why I asked you to come here this evening — I must make it clear to you that she's my wench and not yours."

[margin notes, handwritten: "love triangle ~ jealousy"; ""owned" love vs. "shared" love"; ""owned" vs. soul"; "bad body"]

With that the safety-valve of policy exploded. Paolo sprang to his feet, grasped the stiletto which he had already been secretly fingering, though with no plan of using it, and plunged it where it belonged, in Godfrey's breast.

What happened? There was a clang as of metal on metal. A violent shock ran up the assailant's arm and nearly dislocated his shoulder, as the stiletto broke in half and dropped to the ground. Godfrey fell backward, striking the carpeted floor with the back of his head, and lay still. There was a slit in the left breast of his doublet, but no blood. For a few moments Paolo stood transfixed with horror. Then he bent over Godfrey's prostrate form and saw at once that, though unconscious, the man was breathing peacefully. Cautiously he unfastened his doublet, expecting to see the chain mail beneath it, but there was nothing but a woollen vest. He straightened himself, stepped back a pace and stood staring down at the body on the floor with a look on his face that was half bewildered, half speculative; until a slight stirring heralded the return of consciousness. Then he picked up the broken pieces of the stiletto and left the house.

EVENTS MOVED SWIFTLY. Paolo had not much fear of Godfrey's accusing him openly of the attack, since he could hardly do so without disclosing his own mysterious invulnerability, and risking an indictment for witchcraft. But he knew the man would be out to destroy him by any means that came to hand, and he did not return to the Ironworks. As soon as he could, he told Maria what had

[handwritten margin note: Godfrey can't be hurt]

happened, without reporting too precisely the altercation that had led up to it. Together they decided it was time to take her sisters into their confidence. It was not altogether easy, since Agnes showed a disposition to disbelieve the whole story or at all events its conclusion. But eventually they carried her along with them and the four of them held what amounted to a council of war.

Their first consideration was Paolo's safety. Maria insisted — reluctantly — that he must leave the district at once, go right away and continue his travels. But Paolo would not hear of it. He would stay where he was until the task that was laid on him was finished. What task? He knew now, he said, that he had been entrusted with a solemn duty, to destroy the evil (he had recently discovered that there is another word for 'bad' in English) that hung over and threatened them; and not only them, but their neighbours and all the country round: "Evil ... starts here ... then spreads all over." There was some argument, but he was very firm and in the end they agreed with him; agreed moreover that the first thing, perhaps the only thing, that needed to be done was to rid the world of Godfrey.

But how to set about it? The enforcement of the law was so lax and ineffective in rural England in those days that they had no great fear of consequences. But then straightforward violence had been tried already, and had failed. For some time they sat looking at each other in silence, until at last Paolo came forward with a suggestion. Let us consult your good Doctor, he said. He is wise in other things beside medicines. And when in response to their messenger, Dr. Gropewell joined the conference, they laid the whole situation before him.

They did not know, nobody knew, where Gropewell got his knowledge from. What was known was, that he had read many books, that at one time in his life he had travelled in the East as well as in the West, and that he had met and talked with several who knew even more than he did. All he said now was that he thought they were right and that Godfrey must be killed, but that he must first go home and consult a memorandum he had made many years ago. It was of a long talk he had once had in Thuringia with a learned monk who had been led to Ireland by his interest in early Christian missionaries, and while there had become acquainted with unwritten traditions descended from the followers of St. Patrick and St. Columba and perhaps from predecessors as far back as the birth of Christ and beyond it.

When Gropewell returned next morning he told them he now had a plan which he thought might succeed. Some years ago, he said, in this very neighbourhood, a strange thing happened which people are reluctant to speak of, although the proof of it is there for all to see; and he went on to tell them of a large meteorite that had fallen not far off and buried itself in the ground. He did not use the word 'meteorite' or even 'thunderbolt', for there were as yet no such words. All he could say was that a mass of molten metal had fallen from the sky, none knew why or how. As to that there were different views. Some thought it had been created and despatched by God as a warning or a sign of His wrath, others that it was a flash of

Space iron [handwritten marginal note]

solidified lightning. But the point was not to talk about it but to use it. And he was assured, after consulting the memorandum, that iron (for the metal appeared to be iron) that came from heaven had certain virtues denied to iron from the earth. A dagger, for example, made from it would be likely to penetrate any substance whatever, even the scaly hide of a dragon.

Gropewell went on to tell them that he knew well, and had often spoken with, a quaint old man called Welland, a retired ironworker, who lived near where it had fallen and had been amusing himself for years by smelting the metal from the sky. He had accumulated several lumps of it, but had never done anything with them, though he also had a forge and was a reasonably skilled smith. "We can ask him — in fact I have already asked him — to find a suitable lump and forge it into a dagger. I have told him I want it for an ornament, but that it must be a real dagger and a sharp one. I hope to bring it to you tomorrow, and that will be all I can do. It is for you to make your plans and very careful plans they should be, for the time and place and manner of using it."

He left them then, with his blessing; and now they had their own forging to do, a mental forging not a metal one. It took them a long time, but before they parted, they had not only agreed on the best of several plans that were suggested but had worked it out into its finer details. It had one drawback. It was Maria who, at least for some moments, would be placed in deadly peril. And yet it was Maria herself who suggested it.

"I WILL NOT be seen going into your cottage — not yet."

Maria was arguing with Godfrey on the brow of a gentle slope that led down to Black Hollow Forge, and he was not pleased. But at last her insistence was too much for him, and he gave way. The assignation fixed for the following day would be kept, not in his house, as he had assumed, but in a small open glade in the woodland behind them where no-one ever came.

When that day dawned, the weather was fine and clear, but Godfrey, when he rose, was a little annoyed to notice that the sky was beginning to haze over. The sun still shone beneficently through and it was doubtful if the faint rumble he fancied he heard in the distance had anything to do with the haze. For once the place was silent. This happened to be the date of the annual fair in the neighbouring town and — much to their surprise — he had offered his workmen a half-day's holiday. He had felt it just as well to have them out of the way.

Godfrey was now very agitated. Things kept coming into his mind and slipping out of it again almost as soon as they appeared. He must not forget to lock the door or to open the sluice in the Freeway now the machinery had stopped. He mustn't forget. What was the time? Should he start now? Did he want to get there first? Yes, No, better not. At last he left the house and began to make his way towards the rendezvous.

In a simple white dress Maria emerged from the surrounding trees into the little green glade. In dun-coloured garments, nearly the colour of its bark, Paolo remained behind the largest of them. He too was agitated

— enough so to find some difficulty in doing what he knew he must do at all costs: keep absolutely still. Footsteps were heard and a rustle of undergrowth, and Godfrey stepped from the trees on the opposite side. He advanced and stood facing Maria with a smile that was ruined by greed. He stooped towards her and his hands were already rising to grip her dress, and tear it when he heard a faint noise from the trees beyond. He would have ignored it. What was fatal was the tell-tale twist of Maria's head in the direction from which it came. It was enough. It was the spark that ignited all his smothered suspicions, and they exploded.

"Vixen!" he snarled, "it was all a trick then! Here's another trick!" And at once she was on the ground with his bony hands round her throat, pressing, pressing. Paolo rushed. He raised the dagger and plunged it between the quivering shoulders that were all he saw before him.

At the same moment three things happened. There was a crack of thunder, a powerful flash of lightning, and Paolo felt a shock running down his arm as violent as the one that had run up it when his stiletto was shattered that night in the cottage. Godfrey lay sprawled on Maria. Paolo stooped to roll the one body off the other, and some precious moments passed before he realised that those two hands were still round Maria's throat, pressing it harder than ever in the desperation of a death-throe. Nor was it an easy task to unclasp them. When at last he succeeded and the two bodies lay side by side, he knelt beside Maria — and saw that she lay very still.

THREE OF THE workmen were on their way back from the fair. By tradition it was always a festival as well as a fair, and ale had flowed plentifully in every inn in the town; so that their steps were a little unsteady and their minds, never very bright, were perhaps more confused than on most days. They had nearly reached the Forge when they heard the thunderclap and saw the lightning flash. They stopped in their tracks, but it was what followed immediately after that made one of them exclaim, "God's blood! What's that?"

First a rending noise, then a rumbling that grew louder and louder as they stood and gaped. And then the smoke. "Come on!" one of them cried, and when they reached their workplace, they knew enough of its mechanism and all that went with it to understand at once what had happened. They knew that the dam above it had been built, or rather piled together, with more haste than foresight. They guessed that the Freeway had been left shut off, and that the pressure of the flow down the Workway had been too strong for the conduits that channelled it. When the dam caved in, the whole weight of the water in the pond above would have been free to work its will, smashing its way past every obstruction and pouring itself into the banked furnace. Escaping steam had cracked the roof and walls of the building before it turned to smoke, as the water mixed more and more relentlessly with the smouldering fuel. Smoke! It spread. It choked them back as they tried to get nearer. And it rose above the Forge in a hovering cloud too thick for the rain that was now falling in torrents to disperse.

So extensive was the disaster that no attempt was ever made to restore the building or to construct another on the same site. But when they spoke of it afterwards among themselves, it was the smoke that the three workmen remembered most, and it was that they argued about, one of them denying what the other two were sure they had seen. They were no more drunk, they insisted, than he was. They were not numskull peasants, but skilled workmen who knew what they were talking about. Of course they had seen smoke before. They had seen clouds of smoke before. They had seen clouds of smoke swirled into odd shapes by the air currents that held them down. Just as *he* had seen pictures of St. George and other pictures of the monster whose gaping mouth was the mouth of Hell. But they had never seen before, and hoped never to see again, a cloud of smoke that positively became a dragon before it drifted westward against the prevailing wind, losing its shape as it went.

*   *   *   *

LEONARD BROOK LET the manuscript fall to the ground. For a long time he stared at the opposite wall without seeing it. He was not thinking about what he had read; he was looking into the future, facing as best he could its grim uncertainties. Would Vi come through? What would it mean for him if she were to die? What would it mean for him — and for her — if she only half recovered? The blank wall offered no answers and his gaze dropped once more to the manuscript. He picked it up. So this also was what Vi was like! And now, for the first time he started to think about what he had read. Uncertainties there too. Was it even, in some long and complicated way, *about* uncertainties — larger ones than he had just been facing? One thing was clear: there was altogether too much to take in at one sitting. Perhaps he would read it again some day.

He did not yet know that thinking differs from acquiring information and reproducing it. So he did not know that he had indeed started for the first time to think.

Much less did he have any inkling of a truth it is now fitting to disclose: namely that he had just embarked on a journey that was to take him a very long way.

The bookplate of Owen Barfield from c.1953
by Josephine Grant Watson

CPSIA information can be obtained
at www.ICGtesting.com
Printed in the USA
LVHW030425251121
704363LV00003B/473